CAROLINE JOYCE

PERILOUS JOURNEY

Complete and Unabridged

LINFORD
Leicester

First published in Great Britain

Originally published under the name of
'Shirley Allen'

First Linford Edition
published 1999

British Library CIP Data

Joyce, Caroline
    Perilous journey.—Large print ed.—
Linford romance library
    1. Love stories
    2. Large type books
    I. Title
    823.9′14 [F]

ISBN 0–7089–5469–3

Published by
F. A. Thorpe (Publishing) Ltd.
Anstey, Leicestershire

Set by Words & Graphics Ltd.
Anstey, Leicestershire
Printed and bound in Great Britain by
T. J. International Ltd., Padstow, Cornwall

This book is printed on acid-free paper

PERILOUS JOURNEY

After the execution of Charles I, Louisa's Royalist father considers it too dangerous for her to stay in England and arranges for her to go to the Isle of Man with Armand de la Tremouille, the nephew of the island's Royalist Governor. Their ship is boarded by Parliamentarians who plan to sail for Ireland, but a storm causes them to be shipwrecked on the Calf of Man. Magnus Stapleton, the Parliamentarian chief, becomes infatuated with Louisa, but she has fallen in love with Armand.

1

'Louisa, for the last time, my mind is made up. You can't stay here, it's no longer safe!'

'But Papa, I don't want to go, I want to stay here with you! If there's danger, then so be it, I'll share it with you!'

Sir Randolph Foster shook his head sadly.

'Louisa, child, this is no game. Those butchering Roundheads have killed his Majesty, God rest his soul, and are out for Charles's blood, too!'

'But the Marquis of Montrose is still successful in Scotland . . . ' Louise began, only to be interrupted by her father.

'Not for much longer, I fear! And even if the Scots do make Charles their king, it will never work out, Cromwell will see to that! That man is power happy and he won't rest until he is

1

the true ruler of this country. That is something which I, and a number of my fellow countrymen will not suffer!'

'But what will you do?' Louise asked.

'Better that you do not ask too many questions, then you will be far safer!' Her father put his arm about her shoulders.

'You're planning another uprising.' It was a question rather than a statement, and Sir Randolph didn't deny it.

'Just let's say that it is most fortuitous that the Countess of Derby's nephew, Armand de la Tremouille, will be joining her at Castle Rushen on her husband's, the Great Stanley's, orders. That way, he will be able to accompany you and your maid when you set sail for the Isle of Man.'

'But I don't want to go to the Isle of Man!' Louisa was stamping her small, slippered foot. 'I've never been there, and have no desire to! Now that mama is dead, it's my place to act as the custodian of 'Winterwood', to keep it safe for you if you have to go into battle.' Her fine, blue eyes misted over with tears. 'But I honestly don't know why you have to take part in any more battles. Surely to goodness you've done far above your duty already. After all, you were almost killed at Marston Moor!'

'That was five years ago, Louisa, and things certainly haven't improved since then. In fact, they're much worse!' His grey eyes looked troubled.

'The cause is hopeless, isn't it?' Louisa was saying. 'But you and certain other nobles are just too proud to admit it.'

'God's blood, girl, but what's the matter with you? If I didn't know better, I could almost suspect my own flesh and blood of having Roundhead sympathies!'

'I'm sorry, Papa, I didn't mean any disrespect to poor King Charles, or the prince.'

'Not Prince now, Louisa, King. Charles 2nd is our king, and you would do well to remember that fact!'

Then his lined, weary face softened. 'Or at least you must do so in your heart. To speak too freely of the fact is but to court danger.'

'But the Isle of Man is still faithful to the crown, is it not?' Louisa asked. 'Earl James is holding it for His Majesty, isn't he?'

'His countess is. Lord Derby cannot spend much time on the island these days, he's needed here in Lancashire. But Charlotte's a brave woman, she does her husband proud.'

'And you want me to be her lady in waiting.'

'Lady in waiting, companion, call it what you will. It was good of Earl James to suggest that you go there.' He smiled bleakly. 'But then he knows that you being here is a worry to me. After all, Louisa, you must remember that you are my heiress with Richard gone.'

Louisa's elder brother, Richard, had been lost at sea while serving under Prince Rupert's brother, Maurice. Louisa would have thought that the loss of his only son and heir would have been sufficient deterrent for her ageing father to stop actively serving his sovereign and live a quiet life in the country keeping as far away from politics as possible.

Both she and her father had been devastated by Richard's death, but whereas it had made Louisa long for peace at almost any price, it had made her father all the more determined that Oliver Cromwell and his followers would be vanquished once and for all.

'I'll be lucky if there's anything left for me to inherit,' she said with a rueful smile. 'After all, Master Cromwell is busy confiscating the lands of those known to still be loyal to the Crown.'

'You're a mere girl, Louisa, and even he should know better than to make war on women.'

'I find politicians have a way of twisting things to suit their own ends,' Louisa replied, with a cynicism beyond her eighteen years. 'Anyway, I don't care whether I inherit or not, all I care about is your welfare, Papa. Oh, why couldn't you have followed the example of those gentlemen who followed Queen Henrietta Maria back to France?'

'I'm not going to run away while there's work for me to do here,' Sir Randolph replied. 'But we're wasting time, for like it or not, your ship sails with the tide on the morrow. Go now and see if Jane has packed the garments and jewellery which you wish to take with you.'

'Is that your final word?'

'Yes.' Sir Randolph bowed his head.

'Then so be it,' Louisa said, turning away and walking towards the door.

'One moment, child!'

'Yes, Papa?' Louisa turned round.

'Take as many jewels as you can, take all those of your late mama's. At least that way you will not be penniless should anything happen to me, and should 'Winterwood' be taken by those usurpers!'

When Louisa reached her room, it was to find her lady's maid busily engaged in packing a large trunk for her.

'Why Louisa, love, you've come at last! I do declare that I've been quite at a loss wondering what to pack and what not to!' Then her open face clouded over as she hurried to her charge and drew the girl into her arms.

'Now now, pretty one, don't cry, your good papa is doing this for the best, you must see that. There, there, lamb, use this kerchief.'

'Thank you, Jane,' Louisa mumbled through her tears, as she dabbed at her eyes. 'I . . . I'm sorry! I didn't mean to break down like this, but I'm so desperately worried about Papa!'

'Your father is a grown man and well used to taking care of himself,' Jane replied, her lips tight.

'You think Papa might be all right?' Louisa was asking now, a glimmer of hope in her voice.

'If he's any sense he will be!' Jane replied tartly. 'After all, the fighting's over as far as I'm concerned, and like it or not, the Roundheads have won! The wisest thing your father could do would be to sit back and wait until they fall out amongst themselves. Right then, Louisa, if you're feeling a mite better perhaps you'd be good enough to look through this trunk and see if you approve of what I've packed for you so far.'

'You've done very well,' Louisa said approvingly, as she looked through the various garments which Jane had packed.

'And now, Miss Louisa, what about your jewellery? You'll want to take your diamond brooch and the emerald and diamond necklace which your father gave you for your last birthday I don't doubt.'

'I'm to take my own jewellery and mother's as well,' Louisa replied soberly.

'A good idea, too! I don't hold

with all this melting down the family gold and silver for money to buy weapons! And besides, your father's already done more than his fair share of that. Why, there's hardly a decent painting decorating the great hall and stairway now.'

'Well, in times of war one has to make some sacrifices you know, Jane.'

'And to my mind your father has already made one too many!'

And Louisa knew that Jane was referring to her brother, Richard, from whose death her invalid mother had never recovered.

★ ★ ★

Armand de la Tremouille arrived at Winterwood very early the next morning. Fortunately, Louisa had been advised by her father that he would, and was up and dressed and just finishing breakfast when a maidservant came to inform her that, 'the French gentleman' was waiting to meet her.

9

'Tell him I'll be with him in a few minutes, please, Meg.' Louisa said, and the girl bobbed a curtsey before going to do her bidding.

A moment or two later, there was a peremptory knock on the door, and without even waiting for a by your leave, the door opened to reveal a tall, richly dressed young man of around twenty eight years.

Louisa, her cheeks colouring so that they almost matched her crimson gown, jumped to her feet so abruptly that the cup of chocolate capsized, leaving a dark stain on the pristine white tablecloth.

'How dare you interrupt me while I am breakfasting! I imagine that you must be Monsieur de la Tremouille, and I distinctly told my maid that I would join you just as soon as I had finished!'

Sweeping off his plumed hat, he gave her a decidedly mocking bow.

'Unfortunately, my dear Mam'selle Foster, the tide does not await your breakfast! We have a fair journey ahead of us, and must leave directly if we are to be in time for our ship.'

The colour receded from Louisa's cheeks just as quickly as it had come.

'But where is my father? I must say goodbye to him!'

'I regret, Mam'selle that you cannot do that. He has been called away on some urgent business. Will you please get your cloak, or send one of your servants for it. Your trunk is already in the coach, as is your companion.'

The Frenchman's arrogant face softened slightly.

'Don't worry about your father, Mam'selle, he is doing what he feels he must, but I do not think that there is too much danger in it. Now, shall I call for a servant to collect your cloak?'

'No, thank you sir, I'll get it myself.' And Louisa, her brain in a turmoil, hurried from the room and up to her bedchamber.

'Ah, there you are at last!' M. de la Tremouille observed when she came

11

downstairs a few minutes later. 'Come, Mam'selle, we must make haste if we are to catch the tide.' And he strode towards the door, causing Louisa to have to run in order to catch up with him.

'Sir.' As she spoke, she laid a hand on his arm. 'I think that you know my father's whereabouts and I beseech you to tell me!'

'As you please.' There was an amused smile playing about his mouth. 'Come, Mam'selle Foster, and I will tell you something of what I know during our journey.'

'That's no good!' Louisa cried impatiently. 'If my father is in danger then I should be on hand to help him!'

'My dear child,' he said, raising an eyebrow. 'If your father had required your assistance, he would hardly have requested me to see you safely to the Isle of Man! Now do pray stop being bothersome and come along!'

'If you consider me to be bothersome, sir, then I'm surprised that you allowed yourself to be persuaded to accompany me!'

'I am not accompanying you, Mam'selle, I was going to the Isle of Man anyway, and thought it churlish to refuse to do a favour for a friend of mind.'

'You are a friend of Papa's?' Louisa's voice was incredulous.

'Yes,' he replied briefly, this time taking hold of her arm and pulling her with him towards the waiting coach.

Louisa was too surprised to learn that Armand de la Tremouille was a friend of her father's to make any further protest and allowed him to hand her up into the coach, where Jane was already seated.

'Oh there you are, my love! I was beginning to wonder what had happened to you.'

'As were we all, Ma'am,' Armand de la Tremouille remarked wryly as he climbed into the coach after Louisa.

'Our journey should take some two hours if all goes well,' he remarked.

'And the journey to the Isle of Man around four or five hours.'

'That long!' Jane looked quite alarmed.

'You'll be all right, Mistress,' Armand remarked, noticing Jane's pallor. 'The captain of the 'Royal Charles' is well known to me, and is a most able seaman. The ship itself is most fine, too, which is why we should make good time. Now, if you will both excuse me, I have been travelling for several hours and declare I am most weary.' And a moment or two later, gentle snores filled the coach's interior.

'What an ill-mannered creature he is!' Louisa exclaimed irritably. 'To go to sleep like that in ladies' company! I've a mind to wake him up, he told me that he would tell me something of my father's whereabouts.'

'No, let the gentleman be, pet.' Jane shook her head. 'He must be very tired to have gone off like that, and t'will do you no good to know what your father's about. He didn't want you to know anyway.'

'Do you know something that you're not telling me, Jane?' Louisa looked at her sharply. 'Did Papa confide in you?'

'Yes, your father told me something of his plans, and asked me not to say anything to you. It's impossible to please the both of you, so I will just say this much. He hasn't gone into battle. The nature of his mission is purely political, so he shouldn't be in danger.' But as she spoke, she was asking the good Lord to forgive her, for she knew full well that Sir Randolph's mission was one that was fraught with peril, since he, along with some other noblemen, were planning an assassination attempt on none other than Oliver Cromwell himself.

It was a desperate thing to do, and Jane had told Sir Randolph so in no uncertain manner. But her words had fallen on stoney ground. He saw his action as a way of making up for the deaths of his son, Richard, and wife, Isobel.

'Has papa gone to London, then?' Louisa asked now.

'Your father didn't tell me all his plans, you know!' Jane retorted with a wry smile. If she wasn't very careful, Louisa would have everything wheedled out of her! 'But I think it's possible that he may visit the country's capital.'

'Will he go to visit Uncle Jocelyn, do you think?' Louisa remembered her uncle from the days before the war, when he had been a frequent visitor to 'Winterwood'.

'Of that I couldn't say.' Jane was able to answer truthfully. 'I think it had been hard for your father being estranged from his brother, but he would never admit it, and is sorely contemptuous of Master Jocelyn's politics.'

'Yes.' Louisa agreed. 'I have never been able to understand why Uncle Jocelyn chose to follow the path which he did, I think he would have been much better suited to being a cavalier.'

There was a derisive snort from the male occupant of the coach, and the

16

dark eyes opened lazily.

'What rubbish you talk, Mam'selle Louisa!' he announced quite rudely. 'I am personally acquainted with Jocelyn Foster, and he is the ascetic type such as Master John Lilburne.'

Louisa drew in her breath, and counted to ten. She was furious. How dare this insolent fellow before her pretend to be asleep, listen to her conversation, and then have the nerve to accuse her of talking rubbish!

'Monsieur de la Tremouille, I was under the impression that you were so exhausted that you were unable to stay awake any longer, and yet I now find that you've been awake all the long and listening in to what was a private conversation between myself and my companion! Sir, you are the veriest scoundrel to act in such a scurvy way and I . . . '

'Od's bodkins, Mam'selle, but your voice is getting to sound like a veritable shrew! For your information, I am very tired, I have been travelling throughout the night, and I did drop off to sleep. I think that I must have awoken myself with my snoring and then I chanced to hear your talking about your uncle, and have to confess that I listened, as I have always found him to be an intelligent, if misguided, gentleman.'

'Well I suppose that isn't such a great sin, is it, my love?' Jane turned to her charge. 'After all, everyone is guilty of a tiny bit of eaves-dropping on occasions, and I doubt the gentleman heard anything of great import. And besides, Louisa, love, he is on our side, you know!'

'So he would have us believe! But how do we really know who he is? After all, my father wasn't here this morning to properly introduce us! For all I know, he could be a spy of parliament, he could be planning to abduct us and . . . '

'You are a most suspicious young lady, my dear Mam'selle Louisa! And I grant that you have a point. As your papa wasn't here to introduce

18

us, I could, perchance, be a spy for Parliament just as you say! I am not, however, I am Charlotte Stanley's nephew!' He reached into his pocket and drew out a letter, which he handed to Louisa. 'This is from my good aunt, you may peruse it if you so desire.'

Louisa wasn't in the habit of reading other people's letters, and said so, as she handed the document back.

'So be it! You will just have to take me on my word then, will you not!'

'I don't doubt that you're Armand de la Tremouille,' Louisa admitted with a touch of reluctance. 'But you annoyed me with your rudeness, which is why I pretended to doubt you.'

'I apologise if you thought me rude, Mam'selle, for I didn't intend to be. I do, however, have a habit of speaking my mind, which is something which you will have to get accustomed to, seeing as we will be spending time together.'

'Will we indeed? Oh, I know that we

19

will be in each other's company for the duration of the journey, but once I'm settled at the castle I cannot see that it will be at all necessary!'

'On the contrary, Mam'selle, I fear that it will! Castle Rushen is not so very big that we won't run into one another quite frequently. You may take heart in the knowledge, however, that I do not intend to spend my time kicking my heels on the Isle of Man, and will be off as soon as is expedient!'

'Why are you going to the island, then?' Louisa's curiosity got the better of her, and she continued, 'Is it purely a social visit to see you aunt?'

'Louisa, my dear,' Jane interposed. 'I don't really think that it's any of your business why Monsieur de la Tremouille is going to the island!'

'You are right, Madame, it is none of this chit's business! Nevertheless, I will tell you that it isn't purely a social visit, wartime is hardly conducive to such things! I have certain information for my aunt. There, now are you satisfied?'

Louisa had the grace to look shame-faced.

'I'm sorry,' she said, stiffly, and then spoiled it by adding, 'And now, Monsieur, if you are really so tired you would probably like to go back to sleep!' And to emphasise her point, she stared out of the window.

★ ★ ★

Armand slept through the remainder of the coach journey, only waking up when the coach came to a jolting halt.

A couple of stevedores took their luggage to the waiting ship, while they followed behind, Jane looking slightly ill as she took in the foaming water.

'We'll have a cabin, won't we?' Louisa asked, noticing Jane's discomfit.

'You will indeed.' Armand replied, turning to Jane and adding, 'Don't worry, Madame, the cabins are very comfortable, and you will be able to rest snugly in your berth throughout the journey.'

'Yes, well I'm sure you're right.' Jane agreed, although by her expression, she was far from sure.

The captain was waiting to welcome them aboard, and added his assurances of a comfortable journey to those of Armand's.

'The Irish sea isn't too bad at this time of year, although I admit that today is a rum one for August! Nonetheless, once we're on our way, you'll find that she'll rock less, often 'tis worse when she's anchored than when she's at sea.'

'Yes, well I certainly hope so!' Jane murmured, clinging on to Louisa's arm for support as the captain designated one of the sailors to show them to their cabins.

'They're all next to one another.' The seaman told them, as he led them down the stairway and into the hold of the ship.

'Jane and I won't be together then?'

'No, you have one each.'

'I'll come in yours with you if you'd

rather.' Louisa said quickly, but Jane shook her head.

'No, I'll try to go to sleep, and that'll be easier if I'm on my own.'

'There we are then, Ma'am.' The sailor said to Louisa, as he opened the door of the nearest cabin. 'I trust that it meets with your approval.' As he spoke, he stepped back, so that Louisa could enter the spacious cabin.

'It's very nice,' she said taking in the berth which was covered with an eiderdown of gold brocade, walnut dressing table and writing desk, and curtained porthole.

'If you want your trunk brought down here that can be arranged.'

'That won't be necessary, thank you. I have sufficient in my reticule for the journey.'

'Right then, well if you have all you need, then I'll show Mr de la Tremouille and your maidservant to their quarters.'

'I'll come with you.' Louisa decided. 'After all, I want to be sure that Jane will be comfortable.'

Jane's cabin was next door to Louisa's, and although considerably smaller, it was clean and comfortable, and sported a porthole.

Once she was settled, the sailor spoke again.

'Well, sir, perhaps you'd like to see your own cabin, which, I might add, has been personally picked for you by the captain himself!'

Armand raised his eyebrows.

'Has it indeed? How very thoughtful of Peter! Come then, lead on my good man, I would look at this cabin which Peter Smelt has personally chosen for me.'

2

'You're sure that you'll be all right, Jane?' Louisa asked worriedly, as the 'Royal Charles' made her way out into the Irish sea.

Jane, from the sanctuary of her bunk, nodded her head.

'Yes, love, I'll be fine, that I promise you! Now off you go and lie down before this . . . this thing that calls itself a ship gets completely out of control and prevents you from being able to keep your feet.'

'Very well, if you're sure.' Louisa's voice was still doubtful.'

'Of course I'm sure! Now off with you, my girl!'

'All right, but I'll likely call back and see how you're faring.' Louisa said, as she headed for the door.

Noiselessly, she closed the cabin door behind her, and then started visibly. Armand de la Tremouille was standing but a few feet away, deep in conversation with the captain of the 'Royal Charles,' Peter Smelt.

Louisa didn't mean to eavesdrop, but in order to reach her cabin, she had to pass close by them, and couldn't help but overhear part of their conversation.

'It's true, then, Old Noll himself is on his way to crush Ormonde and the Irish,' Armand was saying.

'I have it on good authority that he has already set sail.'

Louise gave an involuntary gasp.

'Then you mean to say, gentlemen, that he might at this moment be in these very waters?' Louisa's blue eyes were wide with horror.

'Bothersome chit! Just how long have you been standing there listening to our conversation, eh?' Without giving Louisa a chance to answer, Armand turned back to Smelt.

'Now you can see for yourself just what James Derby has saddled me with. A wench with a penchant for eavesdropping and a most unfeminine way of poking her nose into things which don't concern her!'

'You are uncommonly rude, sir! I wasn't listening to your conversation, I was making my way back to my cabin after assuring myself that Jane is settled as comfortably as possible.'

'Really? In that case, why are you asking if Noll Cromwell is at large in these waters?'

'I couldn't help but overhear you. After all, you were hardly whispering! And surely it is most natural for me to be anxious that Master Cromwell doesn't set eyes on the 'Royal Charles,' which by its very name is most obviously a Royalist ship, and see fit to board her!'

'The lass has a good point there, Armand. It would probably have been a wise precaution to have re-christened the lady in whom we sail, but somehow it seemed a wanton thing to do.'

'Don't fret, Mistress, if our sources are correct, and we have no reason to assume that they are not, Noll may well have already reached the Irish coast.' Armand's handsome face sobered. 'God help the poor blighters there, because one thing's for sure, Cromwell and his 'saints' won't!'

'You think there will be a lot of bloodshed?' Peter Smelt was asking now, and Louisa couldn't prevent a shudder from rippling through her body.

'I fear so. But this is no topic for the fair Mam'selle Louisa! You would be wise, Mistress, to follow the good Jane's example and take to your berth, for I fear we will have a rough journey for August.'

'Thank you for your consideration, sir, but I find that I have no need to do so! I am not feeling in the slightest bit ill, in fact, I am feeling quite hungry and thirsty!'

'Well that's putting you in your place, Armand!' Peter Smelt made Louisa an elegant bow.

'If you would care to dine with

Monsieur de la Tremouille and myself, we would be most honoured to have you.'

'Thank you, sir, that is most kind of you, and I am happy to accept!' Quietly she followed the two men in a deceptively docile manner to Captain Smelt's spacious cabin.

A heavy, oak table was already set for two, and Smelt chivalrously insisted that Louisa take his place at the table while he summoned the cabin boy to lay an extra place.

Louisa was surprised by the fine quality of the food, it was much superior to that which she had expected to be served at sea, consisting as it did of prime pheasant meat, potatoes, and peas. There was also a rich, succulent gravy.

'This is very good, sir.' She announced, smiling at Peter. 'You must have a very talented chef.'

'Well, I think you are somewhat elevating Master Whiteway, for he is but an ordinary seaman with an interest in culinary pursuits. Nonetheless, I consider myself most fortunate to have him.'

'I'm not surprised.' Louisa agreed, attacking her fare with singularly unladylike relish, which brought a twitch of amusement to Armand de la Tremouille's lips.

Both Louisa and Armand finished their meal quite quickly, and on doing so, were surprised to find that Smelt was not yet halfway through his.

'What ails you, Peter?' Armand asked, a hint of concern in his voice.

Peter Smelt looked up, and there was no mistaking the preoccupation in his brown eyes, as he pushed the plate away from him.

'I must confess that I feel no great appetite today.' He replied. 'But don't let that stop you, my friends.' And as he spoke he pressed a bell behind him on the ornately carved mahogany wall of the cabin. 'That will summon Jem, the cabin boy. I have no doubt that

Thomas Whiteway will have prepared a dessert of equally high quality.'

'Are you not feeling well?' Louisa asked, looking more closely at the Royal Charles's captain. Smelt looked all right, but then he was sun tanned, which always leant colour to the face and tended to make a person look well when actually they could be ailing. Then a thought struck her, and preposterous though it seemed, she felt compelled to add, 'Surely you are not seasick?'

'Nay, Mistress Foster, an old sea dog like myself has ceased to suffer from such a plaguey thing! Take no notice of me. It is nothing more than a simple lack of appetite.'

Louisa, however, didn't feel wholly convinced, and sneaking a quick glance at Armand, she could tell by his expression that he didn't, either.

'Talking of sea sickness, I should be seeing how poor Jane is faring.' She said, making to get up.

'No, Mam'selle, stay and finish your

meal first, and then you can . . . '

He didn't get any further for at that moment, the cabin door was flung open, and a wild-eyed seaman charged into the room.

'What the devil!' Peter Smelt exclaimed, jumping to his feet.

'Begging your pardon, Captain, sir.' The man said, a strong note of West country in his voice. 'But you're needed urgently on deck, there's a vessel coming towards us mightily fast, and I fear 'tis one of Noll Cromwell's!'

Peter Smelt rushed for the door, Armand close behind him.

'Peter, you sly dog. You suspected this, didn't you,' Armand said, grasping hold of the other man's arm. 'That was your unusual lack of appetite, was it not?'

'I had my suspicions.' Smelt replied, tersely. Then he seemed to remember Louisa. 'Armand, before you follow me on deck, see that Mistress Foster is safely returned to her cabin, or mayhap she would prefer to join the other lady, her companion.'

'It's all right.' Louisa said, quickly, her eyes enormous against the pallor of her face. 'I can see myself back, I know the way.'

'Nevertheless, you will do as the captain says and come with me!' Armand's said, in a tone of voice which brooked no refusal. And he took hold of her arm and escorted her through the open door of the cabin, Smelt and the sailor having already headed off towards the upper deck.

'Will they attack us?' Louisa wanted to know as they made their way towards the other cabins.

'It is possible,' Armand conceded. 'But don't worry, Louisa, I promised your father that I would look after you, and that I will do with my life.'

Louisa looked up at him in surprise. Was he being sarcastic? She wondered, briefly. But no, his face was serious. The eyes dark and intense. Then, before she had an inkling of what he meant to do, Armand's lips came down on hers.

Of their own volition, Louisa felt her arms go round his neck, one hand softly stroking his long, slightly curling dark hair. And then, just as suddenly as he'd kissed her, Armand drew away, and sighed deeply.

'I'm sorry, Louisa, I shouldn't have done that. Do you forgive me?'

'Yes . . . yes of course.' Louisa murmured, her voice slightly unsteady.

'Good, I'm glad, for I wouldn't wish to earn your displeasure. And now, little one, I must go and see how it goes on deck. Go to Jane, she will see that you are safe until I can get back to you.'

And then he was gone, his long legs making short work of the spiral stairway leading up onto the deck, and Louisa was left standing there looking after him.

Gingerly, she put one hand to her lips where he had so recently touched.

They felt hot, and velvet soft. She had been kissed once or twice before, but it hadn't felt like this . . .

Then she shook her head in an attempt to clear it. What was the matter with her anyway, that she was acting like a green girl? Surely there were more important things to think about at a time like this than a brief kiss from Armand de la Tremouille, an arrogant man whom she had only very recently met and wasn't even sure she liked.

She knocked on Jane's door, and without waiting for her companion to answer, opened it and burst unceremoniously into the older woman's cabin.

Jane was lying on her berth with her eyes closed, and a low, moaning sound was coming from her lips. Although the sea had now calmed quite considerably, it was more than obvious to Louisa that her friend still felt ill.

She hurried to Jane's side and took her hand in hers, stroking it gently.

'Jane, please wake up, and quickly!'

Jane's eyes fluttered open, and she said, 'I'm not asleep, I just feel as if all the demons of Hell have made their home in my stomach!'

'I'm sorry, I wouldn't have disturbed you had it not been an emergency.' Louisa replied, contritely. 'Can I get you anything? A drink perhaps?'

'No, just tell me what this emergency is. The wretched ship's not sinking, is it?'

'No, no! Nothing like that.' Louisa hurriedly assured her.

'Then what is it?' Jane made an effort to get out of the bunk, and fell backwards with a low moan.

'Stay still there while I tell you.' Louisa admonished gently.

'I've not really much choice, have I?' Jane grumbled, irritably.

'One of the sailor's came to Captain Smelt's cabin to tell him that a ship, which looked as if it was one of Parliament's, was fast approaching.'

'God's blood!' Jane cried. 'But that's

all we need! Child, why didn't you tell me rightaway?'

'I was trying to but . . . ' Louisa shook her head.

'Oh never mind that!' Jane interrupted her. 'Here, give me your hand and help me out of this berth, I don't intend to be lying here in my petticoats when Noll Cromwell arrives!'

Obediently, Louisa helped Jane from the bed.

'Aren't you frightened?' she asked, as she helped her companion to step into her gown.

'Yes, I'm scared half to death, but I see no point in doing anything other than putting on a brave face!'

As they climbed the stairway, Jane going up first, and Louisa coming behind supporting her, they heard the ominously loud rumblings of cannon fire, and a motley collection of screams, shrieks and curses.

'Damn them, they're firing on us!' Jane exclaimed wrathfully, and seeming to forget all about her sea sickness, climbed the remainder of the stairway with the agility of a woman half her age.

The scene that met both women's eyes when they did scramble up onto the deck was like something out of Dante's Inferno.

Men were clasping hands to gaping wounds in their chests, slipping and sliding on a deck which was already made treacherous by a pink-coloured liquid, a mixture of sea water and blood.

Smoke hung on the air like a great dark cloud, so that it was difficult to see properly, and even harder for Louisa to recognise anyone.

Jane caught hold of her arm, as the 'Royal Charles' lurched precariously.

' 'Tis no good, Louisa, love.' Her voice was grim. 'We can do naught up here and would be wise to return to the cabin.'

Louisa knew that she was probably right, but nevertheless, she hesitated. Where was Armand? Was he safe? She knew that she would have no peace of mind until she found out . . .

'You go back, Jane.' She had to raise her voice until she was almost shouting, so that she could be heard over the incessant din. 'I feel that I should satisfy myself that Monsieur de la Tremouille is uninjured. After all, he was good enough to agree to escort me to the Isle of Man, it is the least I can do.'

'You'll be lucky to be able to find him in this!' But Jane recognised the stubborn set of Louisa's jaw, and sighed. 'Oh, very well! Let's look for him then, although I doubt that there's much we can do for him, or for ourselves, come to that!'

3

It was difficult making their way along the slippery deck, and to make matters worse, after seeming to calm, the sea was now gathering strength again, which meant that the two women had to huddle together against the buffeting wind and the rocking movement of the 'Royal Charles'.

'Mistress, for pity's sake!' a pain-filled voice cried, and a hand clutched at Louisa's skirt.

She looked down and saw a young lad of around sixteen. He was clutching at her with his right arm, the left one having been blown away just above the elbow.

Jane looked down at the lad, and shook her head sorrowfully.

'I doubt we can do much,' she began.

'And yet we must try,' Louisa replied,

a sheen of tears glistening in her eyes. 'He's only a small fellow. If you can help me lift him up and he puts his good arm round my shoulder, then I warrant we'll be able to get him back down below and to my cabin.'

'And what of Monsieur de la Tremouille?' Jane wanted to know as they helped the moaning lad to his feet.

'If you have no objection, I'll leave you to do your best for this young fellow while I come back on board and search for Armand.'

'On the contrary, I have every objection!' Jane exclaimed crossly. 'Your good father, Sir Randolph, pays me to see to your welfare, Louisa, and scrabbling around on the deck of a ship under fire on your own would scarcely be to his liking!'

'You don't have to tell him,' Louisa replied, curtly. Then her blue eyes clouded with pain. 'Anyway, who knows when, or if, we shall even see dear Papa again?'

There was really no answer to this, so Jane didn't even try to make one. Instead, she said, 'Come, child, this lad is losing considerable blood. The sooner we get him below deck the happier I'll be!'

By this time, the young sailor, whom Louisa recognised as the cabin boy who had waited on Armand, Captain Smelt and herself at table, was rapidly slipping into feverishness.

'There, there, lamb,' Jane said soothingly, 'you'll soon be all right.'

They had made their way across the deck, and were edging down the curved stairway when Louisa cocked her head to listen.

'Am I not mistaken, or does it seem to you that the firing is less now? Certainly, there is not so much noise, or we wouldn't be able to make ourselves heard this easily.'

'Yes, you're right.' Jane agreed, a flicker of hope in her eyes. 'Very well, Louisa, when we have this lad safety in a cabin, mine I think, rather than your rather grand one, you may go up on deck and find out what's happening.'

'Thank you for your permission, Jane, although I intended to do so anyway.'

* * *

'Do you know if there's a ship's doctor?' Jane asked Louisa as they laid the young lad as gently as possible on Jane's bunk.

'I didn't think to ask,' she admitted.

The boy, his face glazed with sweat, lifted his head from the pillow.

'There is, Mistress. He is called Walter Stokes, and his cabin is but four doors to the left from here.' Then he sank back down on the pillow, the effort of speech seeming to have exhausted him.

'I will go to see if he's there, and send him to you if he is,' Louisa said. 'Otherwise, Jane, you will just have to do your best until I can find him.'

'I have some experience of nursing,

so if you'll just be on your way, I'll see to bandaging what's left of this arm of his.' She patted Louisa's shoulder. 'Go now, for t'will not be a pretty sight, I fear.'

Louisa wasn't in the least surprised to find that there was no answer to her insistent pounding on the doctor's heavy oak door, and when she tried the knob and found it unlocked, the cabin was empty.

There was little point in going back to Jane and telling her that her errand had proved unsuccessful, so instead she made her way back up on to the deck.

It was ominously quiet now, except for the muttering groans and curses from several men who still lay where they had fallen.

The smoke from the cannon and gun fire had lessened considerably, which improved her vision, and she forced herself to glance cursorily at the men who were lying at her feet as she passed them, just to make sure

44

that they weren't Armand.

It was difficult to ignore their pleas for help, too, and she found herself murmuring inadequately that she would send Dr Stokes to them just as soon as she came across the gentleman. But for now it was more important for her to find Armand.

In the event, it wasn't Louisa who found him, but Armand who found her.

'Armand, you're safe!' she exclaimed, relief evident in her face. Then she took in the powder stains on his face, and the haunted look in his dark eyes.

'What's the matter?' she asked quietly.

Armand gave a mirthless laugh, and spread his free arm to encompass the scene of desecration which was all around them.

'You see all this before you, and yet you ask me what's the matter?' he demanded, his voice incredulous. 'And, dear Louisa, before I return you to your cabin, although even there I can give you no guarantee of safety, perhaps you will be good enough to look above you.'

Louisa obediently followed his gaze and, to her consternation, saw that a white flag was flying briskly in the breeze next to King Charles emblem.

'We're surrendering?' she asked in a tiny voice.

'What other choice do we have? The physician is at this very moment attending to poor Peter Smelt. He has taken a nasty leg injury and I am fearful that it may require amputation at the knee. Also, we have ladies aboard. To continue to fight would be certain suicide, and I promised your father that I would take care of you, Louisa, and that I plan to do to the best of my ability while I still have breath in my body!'

'Will they board us?' Louisa wanted to know as he led her back down the spiral stairway and to the comparative calm of the lower part of the ship.

'Undoubtedly,' he replied grimly. 'All

we can hope for is that it is not old Noll himself.'

'What will they do with us?' Louisa's voice was a breathless whisper now, and Armand looked at her more kindly. After all, it wasn't her fault. If anything, it was his own. He should have known that to cross the Irish sea at this time was decidedly risky, when Cromwell and his henchmen were infesting it like a load of hungry sharks.

'I think they will not make war on hapless women.' He hastily assured her, not quite believing that. 'Regretfully, my dear Louisa, I cannot stay with you now, for in Peter Smelt's absence, I must greet our Cromwellian invaders along with the first mate, and try to secure the best terms that I can. When I know something, be assured, I will either come personally to tell you, or will send one of our men.'

She didn't go back into her cabin, but instead went to Jane's to see how her companion was managing with the cabin boy's wound, and to acquaint her with the ill news concerning the 'Royal Charles'.

'So, you're back!' Jane greeted her, turning away from the lad and looking at Louisa. 'Well, did you find Monsieur de la Tremouille? Is he well?'

'He found me,' Louisa replied briefly. 'How is the boy?'

'Well, I've done my best for him. I've managed to staunch the flow of blood, and he's sleeping at the moment, albeit somewhat fretfully. Still, rest is probably the best thing for him at the present time. I take it that you didn't manage to locate the doctor?'

'No, I'm afraid not, and judging by the way things were up on deck, he'll be kept pretty busy. But that's not really why I'm here, Jane. Captain Smelt is injured, and the white flag is flying atop the 'Royal Charles'. She's surrendering.'

Jane's weather-beaten face paled.

'Oh God! What will become of us now?'

'Armand believes that they'll board us. He and the first mate are going to try and negotiate with the Parliamentarians.'

'Well let us pray that they have a civilised commander like Black Tom Fairfax. He at least is a gentleman.'

'But not part of Cromwell's expedition to Ireland, I think.'

'How would you know that?'

'Well, I believe he is a cavalry man rather than seafarer. And, besides, after his wife, the Lady Mary's outcry against King Charles' execution, he is hardly in Cromwell's best books.'

'Still, their commander would well be someone of his ilk. What are we supposed to do? Stay here below stairs or be on deck for their arrival?'

'Armand said to remain below deck, and I think he is right.' Louisa shuddered. 'After all, there is nothing to be served by going up there. It's men's business and I have no doubt that we will be informed quite soon of what is to become of us.'

'Lord, Louisa, but this is a mess!

I should never have allowed Sir Randolph to persuade me to agree to this enterprise in the first place. I did have my doubts, but then with him determined to pursue King Charles' cause, would you have been safe if you'd remained at Winterwood?'

'I doubt it,' Louisa replied with a trace of bitterness. 'Why father couldn't have just let things be, I'll never know! I'm no Parliamentarian, but I do feel that we've suffered enough in losing Richard and Mama.'

'That you have, lamb, that you have!' Jane agreed, putting her arm round her charge's shoulders. 'Well, let us hope that all this will have a happy outcome, and in the meantime, let us sit down. My old legs are tired from standing, and the sea sickness has fair robbed them of their strength. All we can do is wait, so we may as well make ourselves as comfortable as we can while we do so.'

'Oh Jane, I'm sorry! With all this going on, I quite forgot to ask you how you're feeling now! A mite better, I trust?'

'Foolish chit!' Jane said, laughing. 'How can you expect me to feel better after the news that you've just brought me?'

Louisa couldn't help but smile, although it was a distinctly watery one.

* * *

Being possessed of a rather impatient disposition, Louisa always found waiting somewhat irksome. This was worse, because she knew that what she was waiting for could scarcely be good news. After an hour or so, there was a loud knocking on the cabin door. Louisa exchanged a quick look with Jane, and then got to her feet and went over to the door.

'Who is it? Who's there?' she asked, a slight tremble in her voice.

To her dismay, there was no reply, but the handle turned. Fortunately, she had had the foresight to lock it after she'd come into the cabin.

'It is locked from within!' she called out now. 'Identify yourself or I refuse to open the door!'

'In the name of Parliament, you will open this door now!' a nasal voice snarled from the passageway.

Louisa turned round and looked at Jane, who nodded her head, her face blanched with fear. Reluctantly, Louisa undid the bolt.

Standing before her was a man of around thirty. He was fairly thick-set, and very tall. His expression was hard, the blue eyes glacial cold, the thin lips compressed in a tight, sneering line.

'You took your time, Mistress,' he said, looking Louisa up and down in a singularly insolent way. 'You seem rather young to be Mistress Jane Henderson, yet I take it that you must be?'

But Louisa's gaze had gone past him, to the figure standing half-concealed behind his considerable bulk.

'Uncle Jocelyn?' she queried, her voice tentative.

'Magnus, will you stand aside one moment so that I can see for myself if this lady is truly my niece?'

With a muttered oath, the man called Magnus moved back and Jocelyn Foster stepped just inside the cabin.

'Louisa, my dear, it really is you!' he exclaimed, embracing her before holding her at arm's length and gazing into her face.

'Uncle Jocelyn, you'll never know how glad I am to see you!' Louisa cried vehemently.

'And I you, child.' Then his handsome, but serious face saddened. 'Yet I cannot but wish that it was in happier circumstances.'

'But surely, Uncle, you will see to it that we come to no harm? After all, even though the war divided our family, you have always been very dear to me and . . . '

'Please spare us the rhetoric, Mistress!' Magnus spoke from the corner.

Jocelyn Foster coughed.

'Magnus, I would introduce you to my young niece, Mistress Louisa Foster. Louisa, this is General Magnus Stapleton, the commander of the Commonwealth's vessel, 'Vulture'. We are part of Master Ireton's fleet, headed for the south of Ireland.'

Magnus Stapleton looked angry.

'For goodness' sake, man, remember who you're talking to! And stop giving the wench information before I've decided what to do with the whole sorry lot of them! She may be your niece, but that hardly does you credit, seeing as she is the daughter of that infamous traitor, Sir Randolph Foster!'

'How dare you speak of my father in such a manner, sir!' Louisa's eyes blazed. 'It is you who are the traitor, not him!'

'Louisa, my dear, please mind your words,' Jocelyn admonished, his thin face colouring.

'You are a bold wench! And I like not to see a woman who does not know her place! You would do well to remember that this ship is now the property of the commonwealth, as are all things on it! Seeing as I am the commander, you would do well to address me with respect or, better still, do not speak at all unless I ask you to.' Magnus thrust his heavy-jowled face close to her, and she involuntarily shrank backwards.

'Leave my Louisa alone, you great bully of a man!' Jane thrust herself in front of Louisa, and glared menacingly at Magnus Stapleton.

Magnus Stapleton's large hand came out and sent Jane sprawling on to the ground.

Her brown eyes blazing hatred, she spat contemptuously at Magnus Stapleton's feet as she got up from the floor.

Angry colour flooded his face as he grabbed hold of Jane's arm and frog-marched her out of the cabin.

'You, woman, will come with me!'

'No, no, you can't!' Louisa found

that she was desperately clinging on to the sleeve of his jacket in a desperate attempt to stop him taking Jane away to goodness knows what fate . . .

'Can't, Mistress Foster? And who, pray, is going to stop me? A slip of a thing like you?'

'No, you lout, but I am!' And Louisa saw, to her consternation, that Armand was almost at the cabin door.

'Don't, Armand, he's not worth it!' she cried desperately but the frenchman wasn't even listening. The next moment there was a frantic scuffling, Armand de la Tremouille landing a resounding punch on the Parliamentarian's jaw, felling him like a tree.

Jocelyn Foster took out a finely embroidered kerchief and mopped the perspiration from his brow. His lean face was decidedly worried.

'You shouldn't have done that.' Then he smiled. 'Mind you, I admire you for it. You are quite right, Stapleton is a lout and it's past time someone stood up to him! Nevertheless, he's going to be very angry when he comes round.' He sighed bitterly. 'God knows, I wish it was in my power to help you, but with him in charge, I cannot see how I can. I would suggest transporting him back to the 'Vulture' while he is still comatose, but even that won't work, not since he's seen fit to station a good fifteen fellows on deck to make sure that there is no insurrection amongst your men.'

'But what will he do with Armand when he regains consciousness?' Louisa demanded, her face ashen.

'If there is one thing that Stapleton hates, it's to be made a fool of.' He smiled wanly. 'You were very brave but I wouldn't like to be in your shoes!'

'There's an answer to it, though,' Jane observed grimly, prodding none-too-gently at Stapleton with her slippered foot. 'Don't let him regain consciousness!'

'Mistress Henderson, are you suggesting that I dispose of the fellow?'

Jocelyn Foster intervened hastily.

'No, no! I cannot let you do such a

57

thing! Maybe he deserves such a fate, but you will find that he is popular with his men. If anything happens to Stapleton, there will be full-scale violence, and I cannot countenance that!'

'Yet you would sacrifice Armand who has done nothing more than protect my good friend and servant, Jane!' Louisa argued. 'Shame on you, Uncle! For all the love I have borne you over the years, I cannot help but feel that my father is right and you are a poor fellow after all!'

'I am a pacifist, and a man of God,' Jocelyn said simply. 'I cannot give my approval to unnecessary bloodshed.' Then he smiled. 'However, if you have a doctor on board, I see no reason why a strong sleeping draught shouldn't be administered to General Stapleton . . .'

'I think I know where to find the good doctor.' And Armand hastened out of the room, the others looking after him in some amusement.

It was then that Louisa noticed that Magnus Stapleton was stirring, and clasping a hand to her mouth, she cried desperately, 'Oh Lord! Methinks that the general is starting to regain consciousness!'

Two pairs of eyes followed her horrified gaze and, indeed, Magnus Stapleton was now doing more than just stirring, he was endeavouring to rise to his feet, his blue eyes clouded, but malignant nonetheless.

Jocelyn Foster raised his eyes heavenwards, clasped his hands together, and feverishly muttered to God to forgive him.

'I shouldn't be doing this!' Jocelyn murmured half to himself, but the next moment his elegantly booted leg had come forwards, catching Stapleton on the right side of the jaw.

A look of astonishment dawned fleetingly in the Parliamentarian's eyes, and then he slumped backwards on to the floor, his eyelids fluttering briefly before closing.

'Uncle Jocelyn, I'm proud of you!' Louisa exclaimed, hugging him.

'Thank you, child, yet I have to say that I am not very proud of myself. I suppose I did what I must, given the circumstances, yet I have always abhorred violence and cannot feel that it is a satisfactory conclusion to man's problems.'

4

'You know, I feel very tempted to leave that great brute of a man lying there, for 'tis what he deserves!' Jane exclaimed, with a girlish laugh which belied her fifty or so years.

'I'm inclined to agree, yet it wouldn't work, for Master Stapleton seems to be possessed of a particularly strong skull!' Louisa smiled. 'No, I think we have no option but to have the ship's doctor administer a strong sleeping draft. In fact, I only hope that he remains unconscious long enough this time for Armand to be able to get back here with him.'

The words were scarcely out of her mouth when Armand came back with a small, thin man carrying a doctor's bag.

'Great Heavens! But what's been happening here?' he asked, looking down at the Parliamentarian's recumbent form.

'He was regaining consciousness quickly, so Uncle Jocelyn hit him.'

'Why, thank you! For otherwise I fear that a somewhat unpleasant fate might well have awaited me!' Then Armand turned to the ship's doctor. 'This is Dr Walter Stokes. Dr Stokes, will you be good enough to give this fellow here the strongest sleeping draft you can safely administer?'

'With the greatest pleasure.' And he opened his medical bag and took out a potion, which he mixed with a small amount of water taken from a jug. 'If you will be good enough to support his head, for I don't want the fellow to choke to death.'

Armand and Jocelyn knelt down and lifted the felled man's head, while Jane prised his lips open, and Dr Stokes forced the liquid between them.

The action brought Magnus to a state of semi-consciousness, and he gagged slightly.

'It is going down his throat, isn't it?' Louisa looked on anxiously.

'Yes.' Stokes replied, and a slight struggle from Magnus Stapleton was sufficient confirmation.

'He's an amazingly strong fellow, but this draft would knock out two or more raging bulls, and the beauty of it is that it works very quickly. There now, he's safely out again, so I suggest that we take him to the nearest empty cabin and lift him up onto a berth.' He shook his head ruefully. 'For I rather think that the poor fellow yonder . . . ' And he indicated the feverish Jem. 'Needs this place to himself! And, besides, with him crying and shouting due to the fever, he could well penetrate the unconscious mind of Master Stapleton, and Lord only knows, we don't want that!'

'Will you do something for poor Jem?' Louisa asked now, feeling guilty that she had forgotten the lad for so long due to Stapleton's intrusion.

'I will give him a sleeping draft

similar to this fellow's.' Dr Stokes replied. 'And methinks that it will be highly successful on the lad.'

It took Armand and Jocelyn all their time to move the unconscious Stapleton, for the Parliamentarian must have weighed around sixteen stone, but eventually they managed it.

'I'll go up on deck and acquaint the men of their commander's illness, then.' Jocelyn said now, and moved towards the door.

'I'll come with you, Uncle.'

'Are you sure that you wish to, my dear?' Jocelyn looked surprised.

Louisa nodded.

'Very well, then.' And he extended his arm. 'Let us go.'

The deck of the 'Royal Charles' didn't present such a nauseating appearance as it had done previously, Louisa was pleased to see, so obviously the Parliament men had done something about the wounded.

She didn't have long to dwell on the matter, however, as a tall, thin man with a grave countenance approached them and said, 'Is the colonel still below deck. Master Foster?'

'Indeed yes,' Jocelyn replied. 'But I'm afraid that I have some unfortunate news for you, Master Worthington.'

'What mean you?' His voice was brusque, and Louisa began to feel a bit apprehensive, particularly as several other Parliament men were now gathering, and obviously paying close attention to the conversation.

'Why I mean that Colonel Stapleton has been struck by a recurrent fever, and the ship's doctor, Master Stokes, has given him a potion to make him sleep, which I assure you he is now doing most comfortably.

'That seems most strange to me, seeing as Colonel Stapleton was in rude health when first he set foot on this vessel!' Worthington eyed Louisa and her uncle suspiciously. 'And who is this young woman, whom, by her garish form of dress is clearly of a Royalist turn of mind!'

'Master Worthington, may I present my niece, Mistress Louisa Foster. Louisa, this is Sergeant Jeremiah Worthington.'

Louisa inclined her head, but said nothing, although inwardly, she was far from pleased. This dark crow of a man certainly had a cheek to refer to her attire as 'garish!'

Jeremiah Worthington nodded curtly, and turned his attention back to her uncle.

'I had not known that Colonel Stapleton suffered fevers, and I have been in his service for some years now.'

There were muttering from some of the men, and Louisa realised that her uncle wasn't in control. Oh Lord, but what would happen if they mutinied?

'Perhaps you would like to go to the cabin where Colonel Stapleton is sleeping and see for yourself that he is being well-cared for.' Jocelyn said now, and Jeremiah Worthington nodded.

'Yes, that would be the best solution!

And you will both accompany me.'
'But of course, sergeant, I had intended to anyway, for you would not know in which cabin the colonel was, would you?'

Jocelyn opened the door of the cabin where they'd put Magnus Stapleton, and Jeremiah rudely pushed past them both and went inside.

Jeremiah Worthington examined his commander closely, putting his hand on Magnus's forehead, and peering at it when it came away damp with perspiration.

'Do you, perhaps, wish to speak to the doctor?' Jocelyn asked. 'For if you do, I will see if I can find him for you.'

Worthington shook his head.

'No, I think that will not be necessary. For now.' And he turned away in his abrupt fashion, and headed out of the cabin, leaving Louisa and her uncle to follow.

'One moment, Sergeant,' Jocelyn said, and the man paused.

'Yes?'

'I have been thinking that it might be better if you and your men return to the 'Vulture', for then you can continue your journey to Ireland and all the sooner carry out Master Cromwell's glorious work!'

Jeremiah Worthington shot Jocelyn a suspicious look, his dark eyebrows drawing together in a harsh line.

'Methinks that you forget, sir, that this vessel has been boarded by government, and all those on her are now prisoners of war! It is our Christian duty to ensure that she follows the 'Vulture' to Ireland, where the prisoners can be dealt with accordingly!'

Jocelyn realised that he had over-stepped the mark.

'But of course, Sergeant Worthington! You must forgive me, for t'was concern for my niece here which made me speak so foolishly! You will be aware that this ship was headed for the Isle of Man, and I would ask, nay, beg, a favour of you!'

'I cannot say whether t'will be granted, but you may ask it!' Worthington's tone was grudging.

'There are two ladies aboard this vessel, my dear niece, Louisa, and her companion, a lady by the name of Mistress Jane Henderson. Would you consent to allowing them to land on the Isle of Man as they had intended?'

'Tis somewhat unorthodox, and without Colonel Stapleton's permission, I do not know that I have the right to make such a decision!'

'Oh come now, Sergeant Worthington!' Jocelyn's tone was placating. 'Think how you would feel yourself if your own kin were to be as unfortunate as to fall into Royalist hands! Surely you would do all in your power to see that they arrived at their original destination, where they would be safe!'

'I see your point,' he agreed, albeit grudgingly. 'Very well, I will permit your niece and her companion to land on that God forsaken place!' Then he shook his head. 'Pray to the Lord that

Colonel Stapleton will understand the motives of a family man!'

'Sir, you said that everyone aboard this ship was a prisoner of war, did you not?' Louisa felt compelled to say.

'Everyone who sailed with her, yes. Why do you want to know?'

'Because there is one who cannot be classed as a prisoner of war since it isn't his war!'

'Mistress, pray clarify yourself, for you are speaking in riddles!'

'I refer to one Armand de la Tremouille, whom, as a Frenchman, cannot be classed as a prisoner of war, seeing as he is a national of another country, and, therefore, it isn't his war!'

'Ah yes, de la Tremouille! The nephew of that she-devil, Charlotte Derby! Well pray think, Mistress, what a valuable hostage such a man will make!'

'But that isn't fair, sir! As I said previously, Monsieur de la Tremouille is French. You cannot hold him prisoner when England's civil war has absolutely nothing to do with him!'

'Louisa, my love, do, I pray you, be silent!'

Louisa started visibly at the sound of Armand's voice.

'Armand, I didn't hear you . . . ' she began, but he put a finger to his lips and addressed Jeremiah Worthington.

'Monsieur, I overheard some of your conversation with Mam'selle Foster, and I beg that you will forgive her for speaking somewhat out of turn.' He gave a Gallic shrug. 'But you see, Monsieur, Mam'selle Foster and myself have an understanding, so she is naturally concerned for my welfare! I understand your point of view completely, Monsieur, and assure you that I will give you no trouble. There is just one little favour that I would ask of you, and that is that you will permit me to have a few moments alone with Mam'selle Foster.'

'But of course, Master de la Tremouille, feel free to speak with your lady in private!' And then Jeremiah Worthington was striding back up the stairway, no doubt to tell his men what had transpired.

At that moment, Armand bowed to Jocelyn. 'If you would excuse us for a few moments, sir, as I said, I need to have a few words alone with your niece.'

'By all means!' Jocelyn nodded. 'But what was that about an understanding? Are the two of you affianced?'

Louisa, annoyed to find that her cheeks were turning red, hastily said, 'No, no! Nothing of the sort at all! In fact, methinks that Armand here is possessed of a somewhat vivid imagination!'

'It was said so that the sanctimonious Parliament fellow would give me permission to speak with Louisa alone. If I hadn't pretended that we had an understanding, he would likely have insisted upon a chaperone, possibly himself!' Then he turned to Louisa and extended his arm. 'Come, ma chere, if you will be good enough to spare me a few moments, I have something that I would like you to give to my aunt.'

'But how did you know that I would be seeing your aunt?' Louisa wanted to know, as they made their way in the direction of Armand's cabin.

'I have been eavesdropping for a little longer than you'd thought, for I am fortunate in being possessed of extremely good hearing.'

'Then you'd no doubt make a good spy!' Louisa's tone was waspish, as Armand opened the door of his cabin and ushered her inside. Armand shut the door and eyed her consideringly.

'You know, mam'selle Louisa, you're a lot more perceptive than I originally gave you credit for!, because, as it so happens, I have been involved in a certain amount of intelligence work for my aunt!'

'Goodness! Then you really are a spy! But Armand, that's terribly dangerous! Oh, but I hate to think what will happen to you if old Noll Cromwell finds out!'

'Which is why we must ensure that he doesn't,' Armand replied with a slight smile. 'And that is why I want you to take these papers for me, Louisa, and make sure that they fall into no other hands but my aunt's.' And going over to the dresser, he unlocked a drawer and took out a leather wallet. 'Keep these safely about your person, for no-one will suspect a chit of a girl like you!'

'You don't need to be so disparaging!' Louisa was stung into retorting. 'After all, I don't have to do this for you, I could be putting myself in some danger, and I do think that you could at least appear to be a bit grateful!'

'I'm very grateful!' Armand hastened to assure her. 'For they contain valuable information for the Royalist cause. And pray do not take my words too seriously, for I have a tendency sometimes to try to make light of things in order to disguise my deeper feelings.' As he spoke, he gently took hold of her arms, and gazed into her face. 'You're a very lovely young woman and it would be desperately easy to fall in love with you!' Then he released her arms, and half-turned away. 'But I can't afford to do that, can I? When I don't know how long old Noll will keep me cooped up in Ireland!'

'What do you think will happen to you in Ireland?' she asked now, her voice little more than a whisper. That he would be incarcerated was fairly certain, but if his worth as a hostage didn't come up to the Cromwellians expectations, what then? Would they simply dispose of him ... Oh, but it was a truly horribly thought, and Louisa found that she was close to tears.

'I'm too valuable for them to treat me badly,' he assured her. 'And anyway, I'm used to surviving. Somehow I'll find a means of escaping and joining you and Aunt Charlotte on the Isle of Man!'

'Then you promise that you'll take care?' she asked, full of concern.

Knowing that you care will make me tread all the more warily.' He assured her. 'And now I suppose that we'd best go and find your uncle and Mistress Jane, for I don't want it to seem as if I am abusing the privilege of being permitted to be alone with you.'

Louisa slipped the leather-clad documents into the pocket of her cloak.

'Do you think that they'll be up on deck?' she wondered. 'For I wish to go to my cabin first and fetch my reticule, for I'm carrying a small fortune in jewellery, and I wouldn't wish it to fall into the wrong hands.'

Louisa retrieved her reticule, while Armand observed.

'A most wise precaution! I assume that it was your father's idea?'

Louisa nodded.

'Yes, and I doubt that I would have thought of it myself, for I was too upset at being sent away.'

'And how do you feel about it now?' Then he smiled grimly. 'I'm sure Sir

Randolph would not be pleased to know that his only daughter had fallen in Parliament's hands!'

'But not for long, seeing as Master Worthington had agreed to put Jane and I off on the island!' As she spoke her cheeks coloured. 'And although I didn't wish to come in the first place, I am at least in part glad, for otherwise I would never have met you!'

'Oh my little love!' Armand exclaimed, drawing her into his arms and claiming her lips with his own.

5

When they checked, Jane wasn't in her cabin, but Jem, the cabin boy, appeared to be sleeping quite peacefully, so they didn't linger in case their presence disturbed his slumber. Instead, they went up on deck to see whether there was any sign of Jane or Louisa's uncle, and to find out how closely the Parliament ship 'Vulture' was trailing them.

Jocelyn was deep in conversation with one of the Parliament men, and on seeing Louisa and Armand approaching, he broke off, and after briefly introducing them, put his arm loosely about Louisa's shoulders, and walked her over to an area which was virtually free of Parliamentarians.

'Where's Jane?' Louisa wanted to know.

'Helping Dr Stokes, but no doubt

she will be up on deck again ere long, for she will want to know how you're faring.' Jocelyn answered.

'Did you manage to get any information out of that man?' Armand said now, and it struck Louisa as strange that Armand seemed to completely trust her uncle, and yet, technically, Jocelyn was on the other side! However, he had shown himself to be sympathetic towards them by his attack on Magnus Stapleton, but she guessed that he had had to wrestle with his conscience in order to do that . . .

'Not a great deal, I'm afraid!' Jocelyn replied with a weary smile. 'Although I did try to find out without, I trust, seeming to! The intention is for the 'Vulture' to keep us within sight, although her navigator may wonder why we're heading in the direction of the Isle of Man instead of steering a straight course for Ireland! There again, possibly they won't, seeing as how the Manx island lies quite centrally in the Irish sea, and we would probably have to pass fairly close by in any event! The Parliamentary vessel is much larger than this ship and the 'Royal Charles,' being so much lighter, could outrun her, and possibly this is what your captain is trying to do.'

Armand shook his head.

'The captain, Peter Smelt, took an injury, and the ship is now being steered by the first mate. I've met him, and he's a good fellow, very loyal to the cause, so no doubt he will be doing his best.'

Louisa, looking behind the 'Royal Charles,' now said, 'I do believe that the Parliament vessel seems to be slipping further away!'

The others followed her gaze, and found that she was right, for the 'Vulture' was definitely not as close as she had been at first.

Armand chuckled.

'Then first mate Rogan is doing as we thought he might, and increasing the power! With a bit of luck, we might even be able to lose them!'

'How far from the Isle of Man do you judge us to be?' Louisa asked.

Armand shrugged.

'With all that has happened, 'tis difficult to say! I would go below and ask Rogan, but I have a sneaking suspicion that they may well have posted a soldier there to stop anyone gaining entrance to him. Still, nothing ventured, nothing gained. They may be too busy with other things. So if you will both excuse me for a few minutes, I'll see if 'tis possible to speak with him.'

'Do you think he'll succeed?' Louisa asked her uncle.

'He'd have had a better chance if I'd have accompanied him.' Then he gave a mirthless laugh. 'Oh, I realise that I'm not wholly trusted, but at least I'm supposed to be on their side, and a common soldier would likely take notice of me!'

'Well what are we waiting for?' Louisa asked now. 'Let's go!'

There was a soldier on duty, outside

the area where the first mate was navigating the ship, and Armand was in conversation with him when Louisa and her uncle arrived on the scene.

The soldier immediately recognised Jocelyn, and saluted.

'You will move away from there, sirrah, for there is no need to for you to be on duty, as I understand that the first mate has been acquainted with the vessel's destination.'

'Very good, Master Foster, sir! Is there any duty which you wish me to undertake instead?'

'You could go below deck and see if you can be of assistance in helping with the wounded,' Jocelyn replied.

'Very good, Master Foster.' And the man saluted again, before going off in the opposite direction.

Armand raised one dark eye brow.

'I'm impressed! Obviously your presence does carry a considerable amount of weight after all!'

'Well I was MP for Middleton, and I think that impresses the ordinary ranks.'

Then his mouth tightened. 'Regretfully, it doesn't work so well on Stapleton, nor on Jeremiah Worthington! But let us go and speak with Rogan while we have the opportunity. That soldier might run into Worthington and be reprimanded for deserting his post!'

First mate Rogan looked up in surprise as they entered the covered compartment where the ship's wheel was.

'Monsieur de la Tremouille! What brings you here? When last I looked, there was one of those iron-clad fellows keeping watch on me!'

'My uncle's managed to send him on his way.' Louisa replied.

'Your uncle? Ah, you mean this fellow here!' Rogan frowned. 'You look familiar, sir, and garbed in that sombre dress, I can only assume that you are on the side of Parliament, and, as such, are not welcome here!'

'Calm down, Rogan!' Armand's voice was firm. 'The lady is Mistress Louisa Foster, daughter of Sir Randolph, and her uncle is Sir Randolph's brother, Master Jocelyn Foster.'

'But he's a member of Parliament!' Rogan expostulated. 'What do you mean by . . . '

'Don't take on so, my good fellow! I am but a former member of Parliament. I'm afraid Master Cromwell and myself had something of a falling out over the death penalty for Charles Stu . . . I mean the late king! I am not wholly in his confidence these days, which I believe, is why he wants me travelling to Ireland, so he can keep a watch on me, so to speak!'

'Oh, well I suppose I begin to understand.' Rogan replied, although he still didn't look wholly convinced, and Louisa began to appreciate just how difficult her uncle's standing was, not really being completely trusted by either side.

'You'll have had instructions to head for the Isle of Man to let off Mistress Louisa and her companion, I take it?'

84

Armand was asking the first mate now. Rogan nodded.

'Yes, and surprised I was to hear it, too! For this thin scarecrow of a man came here and told me that I was to edge in as close to the island as I could, and drop off two ladies at a deserted cove, for naturally he didn't want anyone to see that there were Parliament men aboard the vessel. I had thought that I might be able to head for somewhere more densely populated, and try to get help, but he's a crafty fellow, and seemed to guess my thoughts, for that's when he decided to post that soldier there to watch me, and said that he would return himself when we got near to the island.'

'Damn!' Armand exclaimed, in exasperation. 'For I had hoped that you would be able to do something of that nature! And what, pray, is the use of leaving Louisa and Mistress Jane at some deserted spot? They could have miles to travel to civilisation!'

'Well, 'tis not that big a place to

begin with, and I reckon that I could manage to land at Scarlett, which is not too far from Castletown itself.' Rogan shrugged. 'And who knows? We could be lucky, and manage to attract someone's attention, for there may well at least be fisherfolk about!'

'I understand from my Aunt, Charlotte Derby, that there is some dissension amongst the ordinary Manx folk. In fact, I've even heard that some of them are starting to rebel against the taxes which Earl James has been forced to levy in order to equip his soldiers. And, of course, with a lot of Manx people, the former Lieutenant Governor of the island, Edward Christian's imprisonment in Peel castle, has been most unpopular. They think of him as a Manx patriot, but, of course, he was really conspiring with the Parliamentarians, so what choice did poor Earl James have? But the common folk don't stop to think about all that!'

'So there are problems on the Isle of

Man, then?' Louisa asked.

'I'm afraid so.' Armand agreed. 'But my aunt is a very strong woman, I don't think anyone would be brave enough to actually start an organised rebellion against her.'

'That's the least of our problems at the moment,' Rogan observed gloomily. 'For we don't even know how to go about getting ourselves to the Isle of Man instead of Ireland and that butcher Cromwell, in the first place!'

'Very true,' Jocelyn interposed. 'Are you trying to out-run the Parliament ship? For you may have more chance of success if you do!'

Rogan hesitated, before mouthing to Armand, 'He can be trusted, can he?'

'Yes I can,' Jocelyn himself replied with a rather sad smile.

'Very well then, yes, I'm making what speed I can, and I reckon that we should be nearing the Calf of Man in around an hour.'

'So the best thing that we can do would be to keep Worthington out of the way, wouldn't it?' Armand mused now.

'If you can, yes, but I don't know if you'll manage it, for he strikes me as a wily knave!'

'Well 'tis no good looking at me for help there.' Jocelyn said. 'In fact I do believe, Armand, that he would be more likely to listen to you than myself!'

'You could be right,' Armand agreed. 'But don't take it too much to heart, for I rather think that he's terrified of putting a foot wrong in case he should antagonise Colonel Stapleton.'

'And where is the noble captain?' Rogan's voice was sarcastic and Armand quickly told him what had become of Stapleton. Rogan eyed Jocelyn with a newly found respect, and actually went so far as to clap him quite heartily on the back.

'If you can do that, then I'm proud to know you!' he exclaimed, and Jocelyn made a courtly bow, and said, gravely.

'Why thank you, Master Rogan.'

★ ★ ★

They went back up on deck then, but Armand didn't stay with Louisa and her uncle, instead, he went in search of Jeremiah Worthington, to see if there was any way in which he could further ingratiate himself with the Parliamentarian.

Louisa watched him making his way along the deck, and down the stairway, his walk straight and steady, despite the fact that the small ship was still pitching.

'Oh, there you are!' a familiar voice exclaimed, impatiently, and she turned round to see Jane. 'Do you realise that I've combed this wretched vessel looking for you!' She gulped as she took in the frothing sea. 'I suppose I should have guessed that you'd be up here watching that!'

'I'm not watching the sea, Jane, although I have to admit that I prefer to get some fresh air rather than being cooped up down below! How are the wounded faring? I heard that you'd been helping Dr Stokes.' Then she looked guilty. 'Is there anything that I can do?'

'They've all been made as comfortable as is possible, given the circumstances. And in any event, I wouldn't have wanted you there, lamb. Some of them, I have to say, were not fit for your innocent young eyes!'

'I'm not a piece of porcelain, Jane! I'm a flesh and blood grown woman!'

'But a maid still,' Jane replied in a tone of finality.

'One wonders for how much longer, though,' her uncle said now, a smile curving his lips. 'For methinks that the noble Armand is quite taken with our little Louisa!'

'Ah! So that's how the land lies, is it? Well, 'tis as they say, 'While the cat's away, the mice will play!' and I have been missing a while! But anyway, she could do far worse!' Jane looked about her. 'And where is the frenchman now?'

'Looking for Master Worthington to see if he can manage to get himself into that gentleman's good books!'

'What! That sour faced old crow! Think you that he has any?'

'Well, Armand seemed to be making a better impression on him than poor Uncle,' Louisa said now.

'Indeed yes,' Jocelyn agreed gravely. 'The fellow made it more than obvious that he had little patience with me!'

'That must be because he's wondering where your true loyalties lie,' Jane observed with her usual shrewdness. 'You didn't make yourself too obvious, did you, Master Foster?'

'I didn't think so!'

'I think it was when you said about the men going back to the 'Vulture,' ' Louisa said, remembering how grim Jeremiah's face had looked at that moment. 'I don't think he liked that.

'Perhaps that wasn't very diplomatic,' Jane remarked.

'Probably not, but you have to admit that it would have made things a good deal easier for us!'

'Ah, but here is Master Worthington now, and accompanied by Armand!' Louisa said, lowering her voice so that the others could only just manage to hear her.

Jeremiah Worthington inclined his head, and then addressed Jane.

'You did good work with the wounded, Mistress, I would congratulate you on your nursing skills.'

Jane bobbed a curtsey and, keeping her eyes lowered demurely, replied, 'Why thank you, Sergeant Worthington, you are most kind!'

'Think nought of it, You seem a sensible woman,' he said.

'Are we near to the island yet, Sergeant Worthington?' Jane asked now.

Worthington actually permitted himself a slight smile.

'If I am not mistaken, Mistress, that should be the Calf of Man, a small island off the main island's southern most point!'

'Thank the good Lord for that!'

'Methinks that you have no liking for sea travel.'

'No, I certainly haven't! I . . . '

But Jane got no further, for at that moment, there was a cry of astonishment from Louisa, and a 'Mon Dieu!' from Armand, and the next moment, the bull-like figure of Magnus Stapleton was bearing down on them.

'Worthington, there has been treachery and treason abroad!' Magnus Stapleton cried now, and Louisa and Jane saw to their horror that his heavy-jowled face was almost puce with rage.

'Why Colonel, sir, what mean you?' Worthington asked now, his gaunt face looking positively haggard.

'I have been treated most scurvily! By both these knaves here!' And he pointed an accusatory finger at Armand and Jocelyn.

'Well I didn't trust Master Foster myself,' Worthington said hurriedly, 'and insisted on seeing you as you lay sleeping after the draft the doctor gave you for your fever.'

'Fever? What fever? I have not been suffering from a fever! Rather have I been struck about the head by those two fellows yonder, and then forcibly given a potion to induce sleep!'

'Oh sir, I had not realised!' Worthington was clenching and unclenching his bony hands.

'No, Methinks that your perception is much in need of improvement! But there are other matters of import for now! Once we reach Ireland, Foster will be tried for treason, and the French fellow kept hostage.' Stapleton narrowed his pale blue eyes, as he gazed at the horizon. 'But surely that land that I see yonder is not Ireland?'

'No, Colonel, 'tis the Calf of Man, the small island to the south of the Isle of Man.'

'But what is the ship doing here? This isn't on course for Ireland!'

'No, I realise that.' Worthington was practically shaking now. 'But I had agreed that the two ladies should land there and . . .'

'You imbecile!' Magnus Stapleton cried, looking as if he would dearly like to strike his sergeant.

Louisa edged away from the group as quietly as she could. She knew that Stapleton's attention was focused entirely on his hapless sergeant, and if she was quick, she should be able to make her way to first mate Rogan, and see if he could think of any way of out-witting the parliamentarians.

Louisa was lucky, for Magnus was a man absorbed, shouting and bawling at Worthington to the extent that he was oblivious to all else.

'Stapleton has recovered consciousness, and is on deck,' she said to Rogan without any preliminaries. 'He isn't going to allow Jane and myself to land on the Isle of Man. Can you think of anything we can do?'

Rogan stroked his dark beard and sighed.

'I fear that I can think of but one

desperate measure, and I must warn you to be ready to abandon ship! I will head for the treacherous Kitterland straits, the sea between the Calf and the Isle of Man, and in these bad weather conditions, the 'Royal Charles' is almost certain to go aground.'

'But if the stretch of water is that bad, then surely we will all drown!'

'Possibly so. But if I head for Ireland, and really, there will be no 'if' about it, for they will force me to, we could well have an even worse fate! But you must decide quickly, Mistress, for I will have no choice in the matter soon!' The words were scarcely out of Rogan's mouth when Stapleton himself appeared in the doorway.

'What are you doing down here, Mistress?' And then, before Louisa had time to answer he continued, 'Get yourself back up on deck, the woman who acts as your companion is looking for you!'

Louisa bobbed a curtsey to Stapleton, and then nodded to Rogan. Hopefully, he would correctly interpret her nod as meaning that she wished him to head for the Kitterland straits . . .

She didn't go upstairs immediately but lingered outside to see what Stapleton would say.

'You will turn this ship in the direction of Ireland, for there will be no landing on the Isle of Man.' Stapleton's voice was loud and arrogant.

Louisa didn't wait to hear any more, instead, hoisting her skirts up around her ankles, she headed back on deck as quickly as she could.

'Louisa, where in the name of God have you been?' Jane demanded.

'Where are Armand and Uncle Jocelyn?'

'Magnus Stapleton ordered them to go below deck.'

'He hasn't had them locked up?' Louisa's voice was frantic, as she pictured the ship sinking, and Armand and her uncle trapped in their cabins.

'No, I think not, for they can hardly get off the ship now, can they? But apart from the obvious, what's the matter, Louisa, child? For you're looking very pale!'

'Just about everything's the matter!' Louisa replied, mirthlessly, and she hurriedly told Jane where she'd been, and what Rogan had said.

Jane drew in her breath.

'Will he do it, think you?'

Louisa shook her head.

'I don't rightly know, but I think that he might, for I heard Colonel Stapleton giving him the order to turn towards Ireland, and I know that he was most loath to do so!'

Even as she spoke, the ship began to pitch and toss unmercifully, and Jane and Louisa had to grasp hold of one another in order to keep their footing.

'Oh God, what now?' Jane asked, her face taking on an almost greenish hue.

'I would say that we have our answer, and Master Rogan has turned into the Kitterland straits.' Louisa replied grimly.

6

Louisa and Jane stood there clinging to one another as a grim-faced Magnus Stapleton made his way up on deck.

'Get below deck!' he bellowed at them, but at that very moment there was a sickening, crashing sound and the 'Royal Charles' slammed into the Calf's rocky coastline.

Magnus passed a hand across his sweating brow, as several figures dashed along the deck, veering from side to side with the ship's motion.

'No, 'tis too late!' Magnus called to Louisa and Jane now. 'This small vessel will never withstand a pounding on those rocks. Stay where you are if you can, for I fear t'will be necessary to abandon ship.' Then he turned towards the men scurrying to and fro like tormented ants. 'Abandon ship! Abandon ship!' He yelled. 'Have the lifeboats let down!'

'I must leave you, Jane, and try to rescue Jem!' Louisa cried, letting go of her friend. 'Stay there. I'll be back as soon as I can!'

'No, Louisa, 'tis hopeless!' But Louisa ignored Jane, and headed along the deck towards the stairway leading down to her companion's cabin.

It was a desperate journey, for her feet were sliding on the sodden deck, the wind whipping through her clothes and hair. Several times, she nearly fell, but somehow she managed to right herself, and was just about to make her way down the stairway when Armand, who had just reached the top of the stairway, caught her up in his arms and staggered over to the side of the ship with her clutched against his chest.

'Armand, let me go!' Louisa implored. 'I must rescue poor Jem!'

'No, Louisa, there's no time!' And so saying, he bodily pitched her over the side of the ship.

'Armand, no!' she cried desperately. But it was no use, for soon she was tumbling through the air.

Oh God, but I'm going to die, was the one coherent thought which went through her brain, and then she landed in one of the lifeboats which Magnus had ordered to be cast out by the side of the 'Royal Charles', and she realised that Armand's aim had been straight and true . . .

'Louisa! Praise the Lord, you're safe!' And Jane's arms came around her.

'Jane! Thank goodness you're all right!' And then her face clouded over. 'But where is Armand? He threw me into the lifeboat, but what has he done himself?' As she spoke she looked up frantically at the 'Royal Charles'.

The vessel was starting to break up, part of her already under the sea.

'Oh God! Where is he?' And then she recognised him leaping from the stricken ship and landing in the sea, his head bobbing up and down in the water.

'There he is, over there!' Louisa looked about her desperately and then, catching sight of Colonel Stapleton, cried, 'Sir, I beg you to rescue Armand. He isn't so far away, see, he's there, to our right!' But even as she spoke, Armand seemed to be getting further away, the ferocious currents of the Kitterland straits pulling him in the opposite direction from which the lifeboat was moving. Magnus Stapleton shook his great bear-like head.

'Nay, Mistress, that I will not countenance, for 'tis too dangerous. If we are to have any chance of saving our lives, we must head for the Calf directly.' And he gave orders for the men on board to row as hard as they could for the Calf's coastline.

'But you cannot be so cruel!' Louisa screamed, tears burning her eyes. 'He'll die if you don't do something!'

'And so? Many others more worthy will, I fear, also.'

'But you cannot! I won't let you!' Louisa was beyond coherent thought as she shook off Jane's restraining arm and got to her feet.

The lifeboat was pitching unmercifully, and Louisa was trying to reach Magnus, although what she would actually do to make him turn the tiny craft in Armand's direction, she didn't rightly know. Then, without warning, she lost her footing, and with a cry of fear, found herself slipping overboard.

Louisa was dimly aware of Jane's frantic cry and then there was nothing but stygian blackness as her head hit a rock.

★ ★ ★

Louisa regained consciousness slowly. Her head felt as if there were a thousand blacksmiths hammering inside, and she gave a low moan.

'Oh, Louisa, sweet, you're coming to at last!'

Louisa tried to lift her head up, but the effort was too great and she fell back on to the pallet.

'Ooh! What's happened to me!'

But at least her eyes were open now, and they were focusing, taking in the worried look on Jane's homely face as she mopped Louisa's brow with a damp cloth.

'Jane, it is you! I thought it was your voice! But where am I? For I know for certain that this is not my bedroom at Winterwood!' As she spoke her eyes took in the outlines of a very basic building. She was lying on a pallet on the floor of this cold place. It was certainly strange, very strange.

'Don't you remember anything, lamb?' Jane asked now, her voice anxious.

Louisa's face screwed up in concentration and then she shook her head, wincing as she did so.

'No,' she said wearily. 'Except that I know not this place and have the feeling that I won't like it!'

'Well, you're right, you're not at home, and that's for sure! You fell off the lifeboat and Colonel Stapleton jumped overboard and rescued you!'

Jane sighed. 'I cannot admit to liking the man, but it was a brave thing that he did. Otherwise, you would undoubtedly have perished, for you had struck your head upon a jagged rock and you were knocked unconscious.'

'That was kind of him,' Louisa replied vaguely. Who on earth was Colonel Stapleton?

'Where are we, anyway?' she asked instead. Perhaps if she knew where she was, her memory would return all the more quickly.

'We're in a building on the Calf of Man which before poor King Charles's execution was used to garrison Royalist soldiers. They've now all been recalled by Lord Derby, the threat of invasion to the island having receded due to Noll Cromwell having turned his attention to Ireland.'

Louisa's eyes opened wide, and this time, when they looked at Jane, her companion was very relieved to see that awareness was dawning in them.

'We were on the ship, weren't we?'

Jane nodded her head in silence.

'And then they, the Cromwellians, were going to force us all to go to Ireland. And the first mate, I do not remember his name, decided that it was best if we headed for the Kitterland straits, even though to do so would be likely to cause the vessel to go aground. And then when it did, Armand . . . ' Louisa's voice trailed off and oblivious to the waves of pain shooting through her head, she sat up and grasped hold of Jane's arm.

'Armand, where is Armand?'

'Lamb, be still!' Jane implored. 'You'll do yourself an injury.'

'But I must know what has happened to Armand!' Louisa persisted.

Jane, however, had no opportunity to answer, for at that moment Magnus Stapleton appeared in the building. It was obvious from his glowering look that he had heard Louisa's question.

'So, you are awake, Mistress. That pleases me, yet I like it not to hear you ask so fervently after the frenchman.

And so I will tell you without further ado that at this very moment my men are out combing this small isle for any trace of surviving Royalist scum!'

'I take it, sir, that you are Colonel Stapleton?' Louisa asked.

Magnus frowned.

'You know that I am. What mischief is it that you play now, Mistress?'

' 'Tis no mischief,' Jane intervened hurriedly. ' 'Tis simply that my poor Louisa is yet confused in her mind as to what has happened.'

'In that case, I am Colonel Magnus Stapleton, and I have a suspicion, Mistress, that you and I are going to get to know one another a deal better!'

Louisa couldn't quite hide the shudder which pulsed through her body as she replied brusquely, 'I would thank you, sir, for having saved my life. But now, if you please, I would like to rest, for I have the very devil of a headache. My eyes feel as if they have been weighted down with leads.'

Magnus hesitated. True, the wench didn't look very well, and she had been through quite an ordeal. Yet she'd obviously felt well enough to ask about that scurvy fellow, de la Tremouille.

'Sir, my Louisa doesn't mean any discourtesy to you, but she does desperately need her rest if she is to make a full recovery. I feel sure that you want her to do that?'

'Yes, yes, woman, of course I do! Very well, then, I will be on my way, and wish you to take your rest and get better as soon as possible, Mistress Foster. But before I go, I would ask that you do not worry your head about being confined here. I am sure that it will be of a short duration due to the fact that when my men on the 'Vulture' realise that the 'Royal Charles' is no longer in sight, they will come to look for us. On finding the wreckage of the Royalist vessel, they will realise that we are marooned here on the Calf and will quickly rescue us.'

Louisa murmured, 'I am sure that you're right, Colonel, and your words bring me much comfort. But now, as I said before, I would rest.'

'And you shall, Mistress.' And he turned and left the building.

Jane waited until he was outside before saying, 'Don't go worrying about what he's just said, Louisa, love, for I'm sure that there's not an iota of truth in it. He'll want to believe it, of course, but to my mind 'tis him himself who's in a pretty pickle. We're far more likely to be rescued by Royalists from the neighbouring Isle of Man than by his fellows from the 'Vulture'.'

'Maybe so,' Louisa conceded. 'For at least we are very close to the Isle of Man, and yet I would think that Colonel Stapleton's men would be a very well-trained body of men. If much time elapses without a sighting of the 'Royal Charles', then I cannot help but think that they will be likely to go in search of her, and then, as Stapleton says, they will find the wreckage and guess that if we're not dead, then we're likely to be here.'

'Well, I certainly wouldn't fret about it now, for you're looking quite pale and there's a lump almost the size of an egg on your head. If you're not going to develop a fever, Louisa, then you must rest. But first let me get you a drink and some sustenance.'

'Wait, Jane.' Louisa caught hold of her companion's arm. 'Where do you plan to get this 'sustenance' from? For I had thought that this little island was now uninhabited.'

Jane shook her head and smiled wryly.

'For a young lady who has taken such a knock to the head, you seem to be thinking right well! I told you that there were Royalist soldiers inhabiting the Calf up until quite recently and, while they were here, they planted vegetables and fruit. With those, and the abundance of rabbits and fresh fish from the waters around the island, we will not go short. There are also a number of streams, and they are clear and fresh, so drinking water will not present a problem, either.'

Louisa lay resting on the pallet while Jane put a stew on to the fire in the room. While it was heating, she brought her charge a glass of cool water which Louisa consumed avidly.

'I'll get you some more when the stew is ready,' Jane said, taking the cracked piece of crockery away. She paused in the doorway to add, 'Thank God that the Royalist garrison was so generous with what they left here, for otherwise I fear that we might have starved, or at the very best, have been eating our meals off the floor!'

Louisa smiled. Jane was a great comfort to her, always seeming to manage to keep the best side up. And then her pretty face clouded over. But what of Armand? No-one could survive for very long in those terrible waters. And if he had succeeded on landing on the Calf, then surely Magnus's men would catch him.

111

'Here, my love, I'll just prop your head up and then you can have a bit of this stew.' Jane said now, bustling into the room.

Louisa was surprised at how good it tasted, and although her headache hadn't lessened in the slightest, she still managed to eat most of the stew, which obviously pleased her companion.

'If I could just have a little more water, then I believe I could sleep.' Louisa murmured, rather drowsily after she'd finished eating.

'Certainly, lamb.' And Jane held a cup of water to her lips.

Once again, Louisa drank it all before falling back onto the pallet.

'Are you warm enough?' Jane wanted to know.

'Mmm . . . Yes thank you.'

And Jane smiled. Her young charge was already drifting off to sleep.

Louisa wasn't quite sure how long she'd slept but she was pleased to find that her head no longer ached quite as much when she lifted it off the pallet.

Then she caught sight of Jane peeling potatoes.

'Oh, Jane, you shouldn't have stayed in here with me, I'm sure you would be warmer and more comfortable outside!'

'Nevertheless, I had no intention of leaving you! And besides, there's lots of work to be done in preparing a meal for the evening.' She pursed her lips. ' 'Tis unfortunate, I fear, that I am the only woman here, for all the culinary duties are falling on me.'

'Oh, I'm sorry, Jane!' Louisa exclaimed guiltily, and she climbed off the pallet. She felt quite shaky on her feet, however, and would probably have fallen if Jane hadn't hurried towards her and taken hold of her arm.

'My dear child, I didn't mean for a minute that you should be helping me! You're not in the least well enough! No, I simply meant that there are a number of men with healthy appetites to feed, that's all.' Then she smiled. 'Still, in all honesty, I don't really mind, for it helps to keep my hands occupied, and if I wasn't doing this, I would probably be worrying all the more about what's going to become of us! But enough of all this! Let me lead you back to your pallet.'

'No, I don't wish to lie down any longer at the moment, for I couldn't sleep any more. Would you take me outside, and I can sit at the side of the building for a while?' Her face brightened. 'If I sit there, I could probably help you prepare the vegetables for the evening meal.'

'You may sit there for a time, the sun is quite warm and may help to bring a touch of colour back to your cheeks, but you're certainly not going to do any work! I can come out and join you, and see to the vegetables.' And she helped Louisa outside, and settled her quite comfortably by the side of the building.

'I'll be back with you in a moment.' And Jane went inside the building to fetch her motley collection of vegetables and implements for peeling them.

Louisa lifted her face to the sun pleased to feel its warmth on her face. But then her peace was shattered, as out into the clearing emerged a group of men — iron-clad, crop-haired followers of Noll Cromwell, prodding bedraggled Royalist captives along none-too-gently with the points of their swords. To her dismay, Louisa saw that Magnus Stapleton was at the head of the group, and worse still, he had noticed her, and was striding purposefully in her direction.

7

'Worthington, lock those fellows up in yonder hut!' Magnus Stapleton called back to a very subdued Jeremiah Worthington.

'Right away, Colonel,' Worthington replied, and proceeded to round up the cavaliers and herd them towards a large hut which was just visible on the horizon.

'Good evening to you, Mistress Foster,' Magnus said now, seating himself beside Louisa. 'I trust that your rest has done you good and that you are feeling considerably better now?'

'I am feeling a lot better than I was, for my head is clearer,' she replied. Then she looked in the direction of the cavaliers, who were being poked and prodded into the hut. 'What will happen to those poor fellows there?'

Magnus Stapleton followed her gaze and scowled.

'Nothing, more's the pity! For as I told you earlier, I believe it likely that the 'Vulture' will shortly rescue us from this God-forsaken place, and then we will all go to Ireland, and Master Cromwell himself can decide their fate.'

'But surely 'tis not necessary to confine them in yonder hut, for they can hardly make their escape!'

' 'Tis my belief that it serves no useful purpose to act too leniently towards the enemy, otherwise they tend to forget who is in command! But let us talk of more pleasant subjects, for that is one which is scarcely suitable for such an attractive young lady as your good self.'

'Yet I would talk of it!' Louisa persisted stubbornly. 'I did not see Armand de la Tremouille or my uncle, Jocelyn amongst your captives! Am I to take it that you did not come across them!'

'God's bones, Mistress, but you would try the patience of a saint!'

'And you, of course, are one, or the very next best thing!' Louisa returned provocatively.

'I warn you, wench, not to try me too far, or I swear that I'll have you confined in that hut with the other rebels, even if you do have a head injury!'

'If that is what you wish,' Louisa replied, and made to rise.

'Nay, Mistress, not yet! Very well, so you wish to know what has happened to that French fellow and that traitorous uncle of yours! So I will tell you. We didn't come across them because they are dead!'

'How do you know?' Louisa couldn't keep the tremble from her voice.

'Because 'tis obvious, that is why! Think, wench, how could they survive in water such as that of the Kitterland straits? Had they been alive, we would have found them when we were out this afternoon, for I assure you that my men and myself did search most thoroughly!'

Louisa bit her lip. She was only too aware that he could well be right, and her face, already pale, turned even whiter, so that Jane, coming out with a mound of potatoes wrapped in a cloth exclaimed, 'Colonel Stapleton, what on earth have you said to upset my young charge!'

' 'Tis all right, Jane!' Louisa pulled away from her companion, feeling decidedly embarrassed. 'It was nothing that the Colonel said, merely the fact that the sunshine was starting to make me feel a little faint.' She inclined her head in Magnus Stapleton's direction. 'If you will excuse me, sir, I think that I'll return inside and lie down, for I am obviously weaker than I had realised.'

★ ★ ★

Louisa was something of a trial to Jane during the next few days, due to her anxiety about Armand and her uncle.

The questions were never ending.

'Jane, do you think that Magnus Stapleton is right, and Armand and Uncle Jocelyn have drowned?' And then she would put her head in her hands, pulling at her hair with agitated fingers. 'Oh, but I couldn't stand it if Armand was dead! And Uncle Jocelyn, although he was on Parliament's side during the civil war, you know yourself that he isn't truly a bad man, and he had repented to quite a degree in any event, hadn't he?'

'Your Uncle Jocelyn is a good man, even if he was misguided at one point. And as to them both being drowned, well, I for one don't believe it! You saw yourself how strongly Armand was swimming, didn't you? Although the sea was decidedly rough, and the currents strong, he was definitely holding his own against them now, wasn't he?'

But her words, meant as comfort, didn't comfort Louisa who pictured Armand struggling vainly against the raging sea, until finally, exhausted, he had had the strength to fight no more . . .

'I can't just sit around here doing nothing!' Louisa exclaimed on the third morning of their enforced sojourn on the Calf. 'I feel useless, as if I'm not even trying to do anything for Armand and Uncle Jocelyn!'

Well what do you plan to do, then?' Jane asked, with the faintest touch of irritation in her voice.

'I intend to go and look for them, that's what I'll do!' Louisa replied. 'Oh, I know that Magnus Stapleton and his crop-haired followers are supposed to have searched the island most thoroughly, but we only have Magnus's word for that, and 'tis unlikely that he's looked in every nook and cranny now, isn't it? But we will, we'll search everywhere, and if they have landed somewhere on the Calf, then we'll find them!'

Jane stood looking at Louisa, her hands planted on her hips.

'Will we indeed? Well, let me tell you, Mistress, be this a small island or not, there's no way that you are going searching all around it until you're a deal better than you are at present, and that, my girl, is final!'

'Oh but Jane, you know that I'm ever so much better now. Why, Dr Stokes is most pleased with my progress!'

Dr Stokes had been amongst the captured Royalists, and Magnus Stapleton had agreed to him being set free to look after Louisa.

'I know he is, as I am myself! But nevertheless, you haven't ventured very far from here as yet, have you? And when we tried a walk yesterday, your legs didn't seem strong enough to support you, and after a mere five minutes or so, we were forced to turn back.'

'Yes, well I know that,' Louisa was forced to agree. 'But every day I feel stronger, and Jane, you must see that time is of the utmost importance! Just suppose that there is little food on the part of the island where Armand and Uncle Jocelyn are. If I don't go to them, then they may well starve . . . '

'Very well, I can see how stubborn you're going to be!' Jane held up a hand to silence her. 'So I'll tell you what we'll do. We'll ask Dr Stokes what he thinks of your idea when he comes into see you.'

'Very well,' Louisa replied, although she would much rather have set out rightaway, for she had a sneaking suspicion that Walter Stokes wouldn't think that she was as yet strong enough to traverse the somewhat barren, rocky island . . .

He didn't, despite Louisa's pleas and cajoling.

'By all means try a little walk, but you must build your strength up slowly,' he told her firmly. 'See if you can manage say ten minutes today, seeing as you were out for just five yesterday.'

Magnus Stapleton, who had moved most silently into the stone building, overheard the last part of Stokes' words.

'It will give me the utmost pleasure to escort Mistress Foster, or methinks that by now I should be granted permission to address you as Louisa?'

Very reluctantly, Louisa inclined her head.

'Well, it would give me great pleasure in escorting you for a walk my dear Louisa, and should you grow tired, and be unable to walk the distance back again, then it will be no problem at all for me to carry you.'

Louisa shuddered.

'I thank you most kindly for your offer, Colonel Stapleton.'

'Magnus, please,' he interposed.

'Magnus, then. I thank you for your offer, but surely you must see that it would not be seemly for me to walk out with you unescorted.'

'I would have said that the circumstances were sufficiently unusual for that to be of no matter,' Magnus

Stapleton now said, but Jane quickly shook her head.

'I'm truly sorry, but I couldn't allow it, sir! As you are aware, I am responsible for this child's welfare, and her good father would be most angry were I not to chaperone her!'

'Her good father, indeed! Why the fellow is a known traitor, just like his brother has proved himself to be!' He narrowed his eyes. 'I am treating you all very fairly, but do not try my patience too far! You are all traitors in the eyes of the government, and the penalty for traitors is death!'

'Then I wonder, sir, why you should wish to escort a 'traitor' on her walk!' Louisa exclaimed, her chin coming up defiantly.

Magnus inclined his head, and smiled ruefully.

'Aye, I am forced to admit that I wonder that one myself, Mistress! But as you are no doubt aware, you are an uncommonly pretty wench, and you are of tender years, so I feel that although you have been brought up in a nest of vipers, 'tis still possible for your redemption to be achieved!'

'By you, sir?' Louisa demanded, her voice laced with scorn.

'I would say I could well be that man, yes!'

'Louisa, my pet,' Jane interposed quickly before the situation got too heated, 'I see no problem in you going for a walk with the colonel here, and Dr Stokes and myself following on behind. That way you would have your physician and your companion close at hand, as well as a strong man like Colonel Stapleton.' She turned to Magnus. 'What think you, sir?'

Magnus Stapleton eyed her warily, as if he feared some treachery, but her gaze was frank and open.

'That is a tolerable idea, Mistress,' he agreed. 'So now all we need settle is when we should leave.' He looked at Louisa. 'What say you?'

Louise realised that she had already over-stepped the mark, and only been saved by Jane's speedy intervention, so she smiled quite sweetly and said, 'Whenever would be convenient for you, Magnus.'

'Well if Dr Stokes is agreeable, then I see no reason why we should not set off directly.'

'Indeed, why not?' Stokes agreed, and he extended his arm for Jane to take, while Louisa was forced to take hold of Magnus's and the unlikely foursome left the room of the dwelling which was home to Jane and Louisa.

Louisa found that she did feel quite a bit stronger than the previous day, but she was forced to admit that that could have been partly due to the fact that she was leaning quite heavily on Magnus's considerable bulk.

'You are not tiring, Louisa?' he asked quite solicitously.

'No, I am bearing up quite well,' she replied, wondering if she could manage to set out with Jane and scour the countryside for Armand and her uncle the next day.

'What are you thinking?' Magnus asked. 'For you seem to be quite deeply in thought.'

Louisa almost laughed aloud. Wouldn't he like to know!

'I was thinking that it is most pleasant to be walking out like this on such a beautiful day,' she replied, untruthfully.

'And with the present company, mayhap?' he prompted.

'Magnus, I do believe that you're trying to put words in my mouth!'

'Well perhaps a little,' he agreed with a laugh. 'But methinks that perhaps you do not dislike me?'

'No, not at all,' Louisa forced herself to say, while wondering in some trepidation what was coming next. Oh, where were Jane and Dr Stokes? What did they mean by dawdling so much that she and Magnus were virtually alone!

'It shouldn't be long now until the 'Vulture' arrives,' he said. 'In fact, I am somewhat surprised that she is not here yet! Still, I have every faith in my men, they are good fellows and well trained, so 'tis only a matter of time.'

'And what will happen then, Magnus?'

'Why, we will all sail for Ireland, of course, and our noble leader's cause!'

'What . . . what will happen to us?'

'What mean you?' Then a hopeful look dawned in his blue eyes. 'Mean you us literally, you and myself?'

'No, no!' Louisa cried hastily. 'I had meant myself and Jane, and Dr Stokes and the others, come to that!'

'Oh, I see! Well, you need have no fear for your good self, my dear, for you will be my own personal responsibility. As for your Jane, you are fond of her, so she will come to no harm, although I would prefer you to be served by a Puritan woman! As to Stokes, although the man was no friend to me aboard the Royalist ship, he has been attending to you, so I will intercede for him and I think that he will be dealt with lightly. As to the others . . . ' He shrugged his massive shoulders. 'Probably they will hang, who knows? Anyway, 'tis of little import!'

Louisa shivered. Magnus Stapleton was a frightening man. Apart from his huge stature and bulk, he dismissed men's lives so casually.

'Are you cold, Louisa?' he asked now, mistaking her shiver, at the same time allowing one great arm to slip around her shoulders.

Louisa staggered, his arm was very heavy, and had completely caught her off balance.

'Ah, but you are still weak, I see!' he exclaimed, his face mirroring regret. 'Well, we have been out for more than the ten minutes Stokes spoke of, so perhaps we should be starting our return.'

Louisa was only too glad to agree, for in truth she was feeling quite tired, and an awful thought had suddenly occurred to her. Just supposing they were to run into either Armand or Jocelyn?

8

'Oh very well then!' Jane exclaimed, her patience exhausted. 'If you really feel that you're up to it, then we'll go!'

'Well what choice is there, Jane? After all, Magnus Stapleton has made it quite obvious that he intends me to be . . . well . . . something! I know not whether he means wife or mistress, but I know one thing, I'd rather die than be either! And he doesn't mean to let you stay with me, either! He means me to have some Puritan woman, and that I . . . '

'It's all right, I've already agreed that we should go! We don't want them to see us, however, and the way that Magnus is always here looking for you makes it quite difficult to avoid him, so I suggest that we leave at first light, before they've stirred.'

'Yes, that's a good idea. But what of the guard whom they have stationed day and night outside the hut where those poor Royalists are?'

'Well, we have to go outside to use the privy,' Jane replied. 'So 'tis not as if he hasn't seen us before!'

'Yes, true, but we always come back directly!'

'Then there's only one thing for it, and that is we leave by the back way.'

Louisa's eyes widened.

'But to do that we will have to go through the corridor which adjoins the men's sleeping quarters!'

'Then we'll have to make sure that we tread lightly, won't we?' As she spoke, Jane looked down at Louisa's sateen slippers. 'Which should be a deal easier for you than it is for me!' And she eyed her own short bootees with distaste.

'Put them on once we're outside,' Louisa advised. 'And think yourself fortunate, Jane, for they're certainly more sensible for walking than my delicate offerings!'

'That's very true,' Jane agreed. 'Well, I would offer to lend them to you, but I know full well that your feet are a good deal smaller than mine.'

'Don't worry, I've got more important things to think about than whether or not I get blistered feet!' And Jane knew from the sad expression which spread over her charge's face that Louisa was thinking about Armand and her uncle . . .

★ ★ ★

Louisa and Jane made their way out of the building at around dawn the following morning.

Their hearts were in their mouths as they tiptoed past the dormitory where Magnus and his men slept, but luckily no-one stirred, and they were soon outside in the clear, fresh morning air.

'Well, where do you suggest we head

for first?' Jane asked her charge as she put on her bootees.

'Jane, really, you'd think that I knew the place! Let us head straight on, and keep to the coast, so that we can examine any caves or other hiding places which we come across.'

But although they spent the next few hours trudging around the Calf, and thoroughly searching any place they found where a man could hide, they found no trace of Armand or Jocelyn.

Louisa was desperately weary, her feet blistered by her slippers, and her head pounding from an injury not yet fully healed, when, on the Western side of the rocky island, they spied an ominous sight on the horizon.

'Oh my God, 'tis the 'Vulture'!' Jane exclaimed.

'You can make her out from here?'

'Yes! I can just read the name on her side. She's travelling in this direction.' Jane said now. 'And for a ship of her size, quite quickly!'

'And you know what that means, Jane, don't you? If we're found with the others then we'll be taken to Ireland and Stapleton will force me to marry him! And you, well, he said that he knew that I was fond of you, so I imagine that would stand in good stead, but nonetheless, he doesn't wish you to serve me and would bring in some Puritan maid!'

'Then why are we talking about what we already know when quite shortly that vessel will be landing?' Jane asked in her usual practical way.

'You're right, of course! So what shall we do?' As Louisa spoke, her face took on a thoughtful look. 'I think I might just have a plan. Do you remember that cave we looked in, the one which was half-hidden by undergrowth, and is only accessible at low tide?'

'You're not thinking that we should take refuge there, Louisa, are you?' Jane asked, her voice mirroring consternation. 'I know it is somewhere that they would have great difficulty in finding us, but we will be quite cut off when the tide comes in and . . . '

'Stop making problems, Jane! I think it will make a most excellent hiding place until the 'Vulture' has gone! Then we can come out again and remain here until someone comes from the main island to rescue us.'

'And just suppose they don't? What do we do then? 'Tis summer time now, but we can hardly remain here indefinitely, and particularly through autumn and winter We would starve or perish to death of cold!'

'Jane, someone is bound to come here,' Louisa replied, forcing confidence into her voice. In all truth, she really didn't have the remotest idea whether they would or not, but she judged it likely that if they kept a fairly constant vigil, they would be most likely to at least see some fisher folk, and they would surely help them.

As Jane continued to hesitate, Louisa, her voice tinged with impatience, asked,

'Well, do you have a better suggestion to make?'

'No, I suppose we'd better give it a try, for I have a distinct feeling that I wouldn't be very happy placed in some Puritan household judged suitable for me by the loathsome Magnus Stapleton! Come then, we'd best be on our way, for if my memory serves me right, the cave which you speak of is further north, and will take us a good fifteen minutes or so in travelling time, and by then those fellows,' and she pointed in the direction of the approaching ship, 'may well be coming into harbour.'

They set off at a brisk pace but Louisa's efforts were spoiled by the fact that she lost her footing on an uneven rock, and fell, twisting her ankle under her. She screwed up her face in pain.

'Oh lamb, what's happened to you now?' Jane asked.

'I think 'tis just I'm getting over-weary.' Louisa replied truthfully. 'Help me to my feet will you, please, and then I'll know whether or not I've been foolish enough to do any damage.'

Jane obediently put her hands under Louisa's arms and pulled her up on to her feet, while Louisa tested her weight on her injured ankle.

' 'Tis not too bad,' she announced when she found that it would support her. 'In fact, 'tis no worse than the motley collection of blisters from which my feet are suffering.'

'Well I don't think we've got too much further to go now. If you hold on to my arm, that should help.'

But Louisa shook her head.

'No, that wouldn't be fair, you're already carrying all the provisions.'

'Which don't amount to much,' Jane replied wryly. 'I only packed a small supply of food, and some drinking water just in case we should come across Armand or your uncle lying injured somewhere, and in need of sustenance. It won't last us for very long, Louisa, you do realise that.'

'I know, yet I hope that it will be

long enough for the 'Vulture' to land and take her cargo to Ireland!'

Jane looked decidedly doubtful, but avoided making further comment. What point was there? Louisa's mind was made up, and although she couldn't help but feel that it was a rather preposterous idea, she couldn't really think of anything else, so she supposed that it must be worth a try . . .

★ ★ ★

'It really is a fine cave,' Louisa observed when they had managed to scramble down the cliff and into the cave which was hidden by undergrowth.

'It'll have to do,' Jane admitted. 'And I certainly don't think that the Cromwellians, or anyone else, come to that, would be likely to find us here!'

'Well, 'tis only a temporary residence, and when the tide is out, we can go on to the beach, and may even sight a fishing boat.'

'It looks a somewhat isolated beach.

And you must remember, Louisa, that the currents are worse on the northernmost part of the Calf, so I doubt you will find your fishermen here!'

'Jane, you're determined to pour cold water on the whole business! After all, 'tis not as if I'm planning on staying here for long!'

'You won't be able to, we just don't have sufficient food.'

'Well, we'll just have to see how long we can manage. Anyway, I don't suppose that the 'Vulture' will remain anchored off the Calf for too long. After all Magnus will be anxious to set sail for Ireland to join his leader!'

'He'll be far more anxious to get you back into his clutches, lamb, and I'm surprised that you don't seem to realise it!'

'Oh, I realise it! Which is why I'm here!' Louisa smiled grimly.

★ ★ ★

Louisa and Jane wandered over the beach that day hoping that they would see a fishing boat, but as Jane had suspected, there was none in sight.

'Well, there's always tomorrow.' Louisa said philosophically as the incoming tide warned them that they'd better get back to the sanctuary of the cave before they were cut off.

'Aye, but not many of them!' Jane grumbled. 'We've already eaten most of our food, and only have sufficient water for another day.'

'I suppose we could always go out and fetch food and water.'

'Water, maybe, but from what I've seen, the only part of the island which is cultivated is the area around the old Royalist building, and if we go there, then we're almost sure to run into Magnus or some of his men, and this whole exercise will have been meaningless!'

'Then we'll just have to eat sparingly. Anyway, I'm not feeling at all hungry, just tired.'

'Which doesn't surprise me, seeing as how you've been doing far more than you should! I doubt, however, that we're going to have very comfortable sleeping quarters this night!'

'Well we have got our cloaks, we'll have to use them to lie on.'

Louisa was so tired that she fell asleep immediately, but Jane found it difficult, owing to the chill which emanated from the floor of the cave. Eventually, however, she, too, fell asleep, but both women were awake very early the following morning due to the damp air which surrounded them.

'Is the tide out?' Louisa asked, and then answered herself as she scrambled to the entrance of the cave, pulled back the bracken and brush wood, and looked out.

'No, it's lapping about just under us, so I'm afraid that we'll have to stay here for the next hour or two.' She looked up at the sky. ' 'Tis a grim day, too! The sky is the colour of pewter and it would not surprise me if we got rain ere long.'

'It wouldn't surprise me, either!' Jane's voice was irritable. 'If anywhere has a God-forsaken climate, 'tis this place!'

'Would you like me to get you some breakfast?' Louisa asked, endeavouring to get her companion into a better humour.

'There's only some fruit and cold potatoes left,' Jane said morosely. 'And that will have to do us all day, so I think I'll just settle for some water.'

Louisa did likewise, and although she wouldn't admit it to Jane, she was starting to feel hunger pangs, and the time was beginning to feel incredibly long and cold and uncomfortable. She hadn't thought it comfortable at the Royalist building, but it was certainly a palace compared to this! Still, once the tide went out and they could go down on to the beach once more and perhaps head a little further along the coastline in search of a fishing boat.

'Jane, do you think it possible that

Armand and my uncle could have swum to the Isle of Man itself?'

Jane hesitated. Personally, she would have thought that it was highly unlikely, but then she knew very little about the Kitterland Straits. In fact, she hadn't heard of them until the 'Royal Charles' had gone aground there, so she had absolutely no idea how far away the main island was.

'Who knows?' She said, at length. 'But it may well be so, for I am by now convinced that they're not on the Calf.'

'Which means that they're either on the Isle of Man or dead.' Louisa's voice trembled slightly.

'Not necessarily,' Jane said quickly. 'They could have been picked up by another ship and taken to wherever that vessel was heading.'

'Yes, I suppose you're right!' Louisa looked thoughtful. 'You don't think they could have been sighted by the 'Vulture', do you?'

'No, for we only saw her yesterday,

and it would have been impossible for Armand and your uncle to be in the water all that time!'

'Then if they have been rescued by a vessel, pray it is a Royalist one!'

'Seeing as they were close to the Isle of Man, and that's a Royalist stronghold, it would likely be one.'

'Well that, I suppose, is something.' And Louisa made her way to the cave's opening once more, and looked outside.

'The tide has gone out enough for us to be able to go down on to the beach and see if we can see any signs of life, Jane.'

'Good! For I'm fair chilled to the bone sitting here!' And Jane clambered out of the cave after Louisa.

★ ★ ★

They didn't see any signs of life at all, even though they wandered along the coast line as far as they dared.

'I've a feeling that this is hopeless,'

Jane said, as they trudged wearily back to the cave, having collected some fresh water from a stream nearby.

'Give it until tomorrow,' Louisa said. 'And if we don't come across a fishing boat or some other vessel, then we'll make our way back. Pray God that Magnus Stapleton and his men will have set sail for Ireland!'

After another uncomfortable night, the two women were feeling quite dispirited. By this time, their meagre supply of foodstuffs was quite exhausted and they were both hungry.

' 'Tis no use, you know, Louisa,' Jane remarked, as soon as the tide had receded sufficiently for them to be able to leave their hiding place. 'We'll have to go back.'

'Yes, I fear that there's no option.' Louisa reluctantly agreed. 'Perhaps we'll come across some kind of vessel if we return via the coast.'

'We may well do,' Jane agreed, but she didn't really think so.

They were nearing the former Royalist

building, not having sighted a boat of any description and Louisa said, 'Think you that they'll still be there?'

'I pray not!' Then she smiled wearily. 'But I'm afraid that we now have no option open to us but to go and see.'

Magnus Stapleton saw them before they noticed him, probably because he was kneeling down, picking some wild strawberries, and they didn't at first see him.

He was unmistakable, however, when he got to his feet.

'Well, well now, and what have we here?' he called loudly, his long legs quickly covering the distance between them. His face was mean and angry, and Louisa couldn't stop an involuntary shiver from coursing through her body. 'Methinks that you hoped to escape from me, didn't you, little Louisa?' As he spoke, he cupped her chin with one of his great hands, forcing her to look directly into his hard blue eyes. 'A forlorn hope! Did you really imagine that I would let you get away from me?'

He shook his head. 'And you haven't done yourself any favours, either, for I would have married you, even though you come from a Royalist family! But now I feel that to do so would be to act like a fool, and no-one makes a fool of Magnus Stapleton! No, instead, I will do what I should have done ere now, and make you my mistress! But you will have no security, and when you fail to please me any longer, well, then I will just cast you out, and you can fend for yourself on the streets of Dublin!'

'And is that the action of a God-fearing man?' Jane asked, her voice brimful of sarcasm.

Magnus Stapleton turned on her angrily.

'You can keep quiet, mistress, or I won't even bother to take you to Ireland at all, simply cast you into the Kitterland Straits and let you drown just as Armand de la Tremouille and that worthless Jocelyn Foster have done!'

'You don't know that, Magnus Stapleton!' Louisa cried, her blue eyes blazing fire at him. 'You don't know what's happened to them!'

He laughed unpleasantly.

'True, we haven't recovered any bodies, although I have heard tell that there are occasionally sharks in these water, and even some of the larger fish can turn predatory if they're hungry enough, so mayhap there isn't too much of your lover and uncle left to find!'

Louisa swayed, and would have fallen if Jane hadn't quickly put her arms around her to support her. She was still weak from the head injury, and also from lack of food.

Jane's eyes blazed hatred at Magnus Stapleton.

'For pity's sake, hold your tongue, man! Can't you see that she's in a weak and distressed state?'

9

Magnus picked Louisa up as if she weighed little more than a feather, and made for the direction of the former Royalist building.

'I was going to order that we march directly to where the 'Vulture' awaits us, but due to her obvious sorry state, I will let you both rest for a time first, and have you given some refreshment.'

'Thank you.' Jane said and followed meekly behind.

Magnus half-turned and scowled at her.

'Oh, 'tis not for your benefit, old woman! But what use is a mistress to me if she is too weak to be able to service my needs?'

'Despicable! Truly despicable!' Jane exclaimed, but she kept her voice low, wisely realising that it would serve no useful purpose to antagonise Magnus

Stapleton still further.

Magnus deposited Louisa unceremoniously on an old blanket on the floor of the room which she and Jane had previously shared.

'I'll have one of my men bring you some food and water, and then you can rest for a couple of hours. But no longer! For I have kept the men of the 'Vulture' waiting for long enough as it is!' So saying, he strode out of the room, his boots once again sounding ominous against the hard stone floor.

'Well, he's in a pretty temper!' Jane exclaimed.

'He is indeed! Oh Jane! What are we going to do! You heard him saying that he would make me his mistress, didn't you? Well I couldn't stand it, I truly couldn't!'

'I agree that 'tis hardly the most tempting of fates, but then you heard what he planned for me. And I scarcely think that that was much better!'

'Oh, what can we do?'

'Well not antagonise him for a start, I should say. And then he may calm down a bit and be prepared to be more reasonable.'

'Do you think that's likely? A glimmer of hope dawned in Louisa's eyes.

'Well he's certainly a most unpredictable man, his moods change like the wind.'

At that moment, one of the Parliament men came into the room carrying a plate of food and a pitcher of water, which he put down on the wooden table.

'There's some rabbit, potato and peas, you can share it between you.'

'Thank you.' Jane said, and reaching down held her hand out to help Louisa to her feet.

They were both very hungry, and fell upon the food like starving wolves. Although there was only one plate, it was a goodly portion, and they felt a lot better when they'd finished it, and had a drink of water.

'Ouch!' Louisa exclaimed, as she stood up.

'What's the matter?' Jane asked, her voice concerned.

'Oh, it doesn't matter! I've got more to worry me than them!'

'Nonetheless, 'tis a fair track across the island, and no doubt you will find it easier if they are attended to.'

Jane was quite horrified by the condition of Louisa's feet. They were covered in blisters, and in some places the skin had rubbed raw, and bled.

She managed to make them considerably more comfortable, but it was quite apparent that Louisa's thin slippers were pitifully inadequate for a journey of the nature which they would shortly be undertaking.

'I'll tell you what, I'll tear a few strips from my petticoats and then bind them around your feet, that should help to make up for where your slippers have worn through.'

Louisa smiled her gratitude.

'We're in a desperate plight, but the

only good thing about it is that I have you with me, for I'd truly hate to be here alone.'

And then they both fell silent, as each wondered whether the cruel and distinctly mercurial Magnus Stapleton would carry out his threat to cast Jane into the waters of the Kitterland sound . . .

★ ★ ★

Magnus Stapleton appeared in the room where Louisa and Jane were resting a couple of hours later.

'Well, are you two ladies ready?' he asked, and they were both surprised to hear that his voice was quite jovial.

'As ready as ever.' Jane replied laconically.

Magnus made no answer, for his gaze was upon Louisa's feet, swaddled in pieces of Jane's petticoats.

'What ails your feet?' he asked, his tone solicitous.

'They are sore and blistered.'

'I wish that I had known, for I would have sent Walter Stokes to attend you. Would you like him to yet?'

'No, thank you. Jane has made a very good job of dressing them for me.'

He bowed clumsily in Jane's direction.

'My thanks, mistress.' And then he leaned down and extended his arm to Louisa. 'Permit me to assist you up.'

Louisa had no option but to take hold of his proffered arm. At least he appeared to be in a good humour, which boded better for herself and Jane.

They made their way outside, Magnus keeping hold of Louisa's arm, to where the small group of Parliament men were guarding the few Royalist survivors they had captured.

'Right then, we will commence our journey across the island to where the 'Vulture' awaits us,' Magnus told Worthington and the other men.

'Not before time, neither!' One of the Parliamentarians muttered only to be rebuked by Jeremiah Worthington, who threw an anxious look in his commander's direction. But Stapleton appeared not to have heard, as he led the way, Louisa at his side, and Jane at her other side.

'You are limping, Louisa, my dear,' he said now. 'I hope that I am not walking too quickly for you?'

'I can manage at the moment,' Louisa replied truthfully. 'But for how long I will be able to maintain this pace, I don't rightly know.'

'Well there is no need for you to, for 'tis no hardship for me to carry you.' And without waiting for her reply, her swung her up into his arms.

Admittedly it was easier than walking, but Louisa felt decidedly conspicuous and embarrassed being carried along by the Parliamentary colonel.

'Really, there is no need . . . ' she began, but Stapleton caught her short with, 'On the contrary, I would say that there is every need, and you're so light that I find no difficulty at all in carrying you.'

156

Louise didn't answer, for in truth, she doubted that anything she said would make Magnus Stapleton release her.

They were certainly covering the ground much quicker now, and Louisa guessed that they would reach the other coast in less than an hour. It was a depressing thought, for she couldn't help but feel that her future was destined to be highly unpleasant . . .

And then her troubled thoughts were interrupted by the sound of pistol shots, and she rapidly found herself back on her feet, Magnus looking around him with the fixed expression of an enraged bull.

'Who the devil is that?' he demanded, but there didn't appear to be anyone in sight. And then more shots rang out, and one of the Parliament men fell to the ground, clutching at his belly.

'By God! But we're being ambushed!' Magnus cried now. 'You, Louisa, and your woman, get yourselves hidden down behind yonder bushes.' And he indicated some bushes on their left.

Louisa and Jane hastened to obey, their hearts beating wildly, with a mixture of fear and excitement. Were they going to be rescued after all?

'Put down your weapons at once, for you are surrounded!' Louisa recognised the heart-stoppingly familiar voice. It was Armand.

She made to get to her feet, but Jane pulled her back down and, putting a finger to her lips, shook her head.

'No, don't make any sound until you see what's happening!' she cautioned, and Louisa reluctantly obeyed.

'Never!' Magnus Stapleton cried. 'Men, train your muskets and fire!'

It was an impossible command, for the Royalists had the advantage of surprise, and it was also impossible to be sure of their whereabouts. Magnus's men, however, were well-trained, and hastened to do his bidding. In doing so, they couldn't guard their Royalist prisoners, who immediately turned on them.

The Parliamentarians soon realised that they were hopelessly outnumbered, and Jeremiah Worthington produced a white handkerchief, which he waved in the air.

'Stop firing, I pray you! We surrender!'

'No, you mealy-mouthed fool! Men, continue to fire!' Magnus Stapleton was beside himself with rage, but his words were to no avail. For seeing that they had no hope of victory, the Parliament men, led by Worthington, were soon fleeing.

Magnus stepped into the centre of the clearing, and his face contorted with fury, screamed, 'Kill me then, you poxy knaves!' And he stretched his arms wide, leaving his chest an open target for anyone wishing to do so.

'I would not kill you in cold blood,' Armand said, stepping forward. 'Instead, I would challenge you to a duel! If you win, you shall have your life, and go free.'

'So be it,' Magnus said grudgingly, realising that with his men gone, he really had little choice.

'I must go to him, Jane! I must go to him!' Louisa cried straining against her companion's arm. 'Why, he doesn't even realise yet that I am here, doesn't know that I'm alive and . . . '

'Louise, will you be quiet!' Jane's voice was impatient. 'Are you trying to get him killed? For Armand to see you now would be merely to distract him, and surely you don't want that?'

Louisa was forced to admit that Jane was right, but it was still extremely difficult to just crouch there doing nothing when Armand would be fighting that great brute of a man whom she knew would show him no mercy . . .

'We should have seconds,' Armand was saying now. 'And as all your men have departed, Worthington, I must, perforce, offer you one of mine!'

'Thank you no!' Magnus spat disparagingly on the ground. I would not stoop so low as to have some

Royalist scum second me!'

'As you wish, sir!' Armand shrugged. 'But we must at least have someone here who will tell us when to commence.'

'Just draw your sword, man, and get on with it!' Magnus ground out the words. 'Or are you so lily-livered that you are still yet trying to back down!'

'I verily swear that you would try the patience of a saint! So be it.' And Armand drew his sword from its scabbard, and the duel commenced.

Louisa put her hands to her ears, the sound of steel crashing against steel was making her feel quite ill. Oh, why had Armand had to act in such a gentlemanly manner and challenge that uncouth fellow to a duel when he could have just captured him? Then she smiled ruefully. But then, the action was typical of Armand, which was probably one of the reasons why she loved him so much . . .

And then the unthinkable happened. Magnus Stapleton's sword darted forward like a slithering snake and punctured Armand's shoulder.

'Oh no!' Louisa cried and, shaking Jane's hand free from her arm, dashed forward into the clearing. 'Armand, my love! How badly hurt are you?' And then she was at his side, her arms going about him.

'Louise my love, not now!' Armand said, as he gently put her from him, all the while gazing at her with love in his dark eyes.

Magnus gave an almost inhuman howl of fury, and plunged his sword into Armand's hapless body, wounding him in the area of the ribs.

'You scurvy knave! Only a creature like you would stoop so low as to stab a man when he is temporarily distracted!' Louisa rounded on Magnus like a fury, pummelling his hard body with her fists.

'Get away from me, wench, before I really lose my temper and do you injury!' And Magnus pushed her away from him so roughly that she lost her balance and went tumbling headlong into the grass.

Armand had dropped his sword after Magnus had wounded him again, and he now realised that this was not the occasion to adhere to the 'niceties' of duelling. While Louisa was pummelling Magnus, and making a fair job of it, too, he picked up a large boulder, and when the Roundhead put her from him with such force that he sent her toppling, Armand was ready, and brought the boulder crashing down on Stapleton's head with the last of his failing strength, felling the Roundhead.

'Pick him up!' he shouted to his men, and then everything seemed to grow dim before his eyes, and he fell to the ground himself.

Louisa was immediately on her feet, and rushing over to Armand, knelt down by his side, cradling his head in her arms.

'Oh Armand! Armand! Speak to me, please!' she implored, scarcely aware of what she was saying.

'Move away please, mistress, for he is sorely wounded, and we will have to carry him back to the ship.' A young fresh-faced fellow with long golden ringlets said gently.

'He's not dead?' Louise looked up at him with stricken eyes.

'No, no! But the sooner we get him to the ship, and he gets medical treatment, the better it will be!'

Louisa didn't want to move away from Armand, he looked so pale and helpless, but she knew that the young Cavalier was right, and if he was to make a successful recovery, then he needed attention most urgently.

'Come, walk along with me, lamb.' Jane was saying now, putting a comforting arm around her charge's shoulders. And they trudged along in the wake of the Royalist soldiers.

'Will he live, Jane! Oh, but he looked so pale, so totally bloodless! And 'tis all my fault. I should have listened to you when you told me to stay back and not interfere!'

'Well I tried to stop you, but you wouldn't listen to me!' Jane replied dryly. 'Mind you, I can't find it in my heart to blame you, for you were under great stress and provocation when you saw that brute of a man Magnus Stapleton wounding him in the shoulder.'

'I just couldn't stand it, Louisa admitted dolefully. 'I wanted to rush in and do something to help.'

'You must remember that you're but a slip of a girl where he is a hulking man, why the fellow must be all of six foot four inches!'

'Where are we going to anyway, Jane?' Louisa asked now looking about her for the first time. 'For if I am not very much mistaken, this is the very same route that the parliament men would have taken!'

'Then no doubt their vessel is anchored on the calmer West side.'

'But what of the 'Vulture'?'

A fellow walking slightly ahead of them overheard and, turning round, said, 'We've sent that sour looking lady scuttling off with her tail between her legs!'

'Oh, then the Parliament men who fled when the shots rang out have no way of getting off the island!'

The man shook his head.

'Any we come across we'll probably round up and take to the main island as prisoners, but the others will have to just stay put here and live on their berries until someone sees fit to rescue them — if someone does!'

Louise shuddered. War was certainly a merciless business, and she would be glad when the hostilities finally finished and they could live in peace.

Live in peace! Her eyes looked ahead to where three of the Royalists were carrying Armand as gently as possible.

He was still unconscious, and probably that was a blessing, for at least he wouldn't be feeling any pain.

But would he come through it? Louisa clasped her hands together and found herself quietly murmuring prayers for his well-being.

'Don't worry, Louisa, love, your Armand is a strong man, I'm sure that smile.

'Yes,' she said. 'And he did say that he was a survivor, didn't he? So let's just pray God that he's right and he is!

10

They left for the neighbouring Isle of Man in a vessel approximately of the size of the wrecked 'Royal Charles', but it was a far milder day than when the 'Royal Charles' had gone aground, and besides, they were sailing from the Calf's much calmer side, which meant that they wouldn't have to pass through such treacherous waters.

Armand was taken to a cabin, and Dr Stokes went immediately to attend to him. Louisa had wanted to go to, but Stokes had gently shook his head.

'No, my dear, you are too directly involved, and without intending to be rude, I fear that you would only hamper my work.'

'Perhaps I might be of assistance to you?' Jane suggested.

'Well, my doctor's bag has been lost due to what we've been through, but they do keep medical supplies on the ship. Get one of the men to show you where they are, and then bring them to me. You will find us in the cabin at the bottom of the stairway.'

Jane quickly found a sailor to show her where the supplies were. Louisa insisting on accompanying her, and waiting at the bottom of the stairway outside the cabin.

Jane shook her head worriedly.

'I'm not happy about you being there so if Dr Stokes doesn't feel that I can do anything to help, I'll come out to you directly, and we can either sit in one of the other cabins or go up on deck.'

'Don't hurry on my account if you can be of any assistance to the doctor, for I'm all right here.' Louisa's eyes misted over with tears. 'I don't know whether you understand or not, but I just feel slightly better for knowing that at least I'm near him.'

Jane nodded and patted her hand, before knocking on the door of the cabin, and at Walter Stoke's call of 'Come in,' she hurriedly entered and closed the door softly behind her, without affording Louisa a look at the patient. She wasn't trying to be unkind, she just felt that it was better for her young charge not to see Armand when he was obviously sorely wounded.

Louisa paced up and down outside the door, cursing her inability to help. In her heart, she knew that Stokes was right, she was too directly involved to be of much assistance. Nonetheless, it was a very trying time, waiting for news. Fortunately, however, it wasn't too long in coming, for the door opened, and Jane came out, and taking hold of Louisa's arm, led her to an adjoining cabin, which she had been informed was empty.

'Well how is he?' Louisa asked, her eyes wild with anxiety.

'As comfortable as can be expected, and still, fortunately, unconscious.'

'Is that a good sign?' Louisa frowned.

'Well 'tis better seeing as we only

have the most basic medical supplies on the ship.'

'Oh Jane, is he going to recover?'

'I see no reason why he shouldn't! After all, he's young and strong, and has everything to live for.'

' 'Tis all my fault! Oh why did I interfere!' Louisa put her head in her hands.

'Stop blaming yourself, Louisa! After all, you could look at it in a different light and say that if you hadn't, then Armand wouldn't have been able to pick up that boulder and bring it down on Magnus Stapleton's head!'

'Yes, I suppose you're right,' Louisa agreed despondently, but Jane was only too aware that she still blamed herself.

★ ★ ★

They arrived at Castletown harbour, where there were coaches waiting to take them to Castle Rushen, the home of the Countess of Derby.

In normal circumstances, Louisa

would have been nervous about meeting this formidable lady, but she was so worried about Armand, that she didn't even give it a thought.

Neither did the castle impress her, although it was a most impressive place, and James Derby had had it extensively redecorated in honour of his Countess shortly after their wedding.

Louisa and Jane were taken up to their respective bed chambers by a maidservant, and then brought water for washing, and a complete change of clothing each.

'The Countess thought as how you'd be needing something new to wear after having been stuck on the Calf for some days,' A pretty, dark-eyed maid told Louisa.

'But how did she know what size?' Louisa asked in surprise.

'Well I did hear that Master Armand gave her an idea of what sizes you two ladies would be needing.'

Armand! How was he now?

'Do you know how Monsieur Armand

is?' Louisa found herself asking, but the girl shook her head.

'I reckon that I could find out for you, though, if you want me to.'

'Yes, please, I'd like that very much!'

The maid bobbed a curtsey, and went off to do Louisa's bidding, returning several minutes later to say that Armand was comfortably abed, and being attended to by her ladyship's personal physician.

'Don't worry, Mistress, for he will certainly get the best of care,' she added.

Louisa thanked her, and then dismissed her while she washed and changed into the new clothes. She had just finished dressing, when there was a tap on the door, and the maid who had attended her previously, entered and told her that Lady Derby would like to see her in her private study.

'I'll take you there now, mistress, if you're ready.'

Louisa gave a quick glance at her reflection in the mirror. Her cheeks were somewhat pale, and her hair would have benefited from washing, but the gown, a topaz satin, was certainly attractive enough.

'If you like mistress, I could re-arrange your hair slightly for you,' the maid said.

'Does it look that bad?' Louisa asked, with a wan smile.

'No, no! Not at all!' The servant blushed. 'But I just fancied that you were looking at it as if it didn't quite please you, that's all.'

'It's a mess,' Louisa said, sinking down on the dressing table chair. 'And yes, thank you . . . What is your name?'

'Lucy, mistress.'

'Well thank you, Lucy. I would appreciate your ministrations.'

Despite not being able to show any real interest, Louisa had to admit that her hair did look considerably better after Lucy's attentions, and she was quick, too, which meant that Louisa was entering Charlotte Derby's private study a little over ten minutes later.

Louisa curtsied.

'No, please, I don't want ceremony!' Charlotte exclaimed, coming to Louisa's side, and embracing her.

'I have something for you, Lady Derby,' Louisa said now, and drew out the leather wallet containing the letters which Armand had entrusted to her. As she did so, she felt her eyes blurring with tears, and half turned away so that the countess wouldn't notice.

'Thank you so much, my dear,' she said, putting an arm around Louisa's shoulders and drawing her towards an ornate gold brocade sofa. 'Do, I pray you, sit down here beside me, and try not to upset yourself too much, for I assure you that my nephew is receiving the best of attention, and his physicians tell me that they are hopeful of a complete recovery.'

Louisa sat down, Charlotte beside her, and looked into the older woman's face. Charlotte was no beauty, but she did look honest and kind.

'You think that he'll live, then?' Louisa's voice was scarcely more than a whisper, as if she was frightened to actually say the words out loud.

'He's quite a tough fellow, is my nephew, Mam'selle Foster! 'T'will take more than a couple of sword thrusts from some lout of a Roundhead to kill the son of my late brother, Henri de la Tremouille!' As she spoke, she took hold of one of Louisa's hands, and pressed it warmly. 'But I am very proud of you, my dear! You cannot know how much you have helped the cause by bringing these letters to me!'

'I am grateful to have been of service, Ma'am.' Louisa replied gravely.

'Those who serve me well shall have their reward,' Charlotte Derby now said. 'Wait there a moment, if you please, for I have two gentlemen I would have you meet.' And then, before Louisa could question her, she stood up and walked over to the door on her left, which she opened, and called inside to the occupants of the room.

'Pray come in now, for Mam'selle Louisa is waiting to see you.'

Louisa got to her feet, all the colour draining out of her face as her father and Uncle Jocelyn came into the room.

'My dearest child!' Sir Randolph exclaimed, drawing his daughter into a close embrace. 'It is wonderful to see you again!'

'Papa, what are you doing here?' Louisa asked, wide-eyed.

'I have stopped off here on my way to Ireland in order to see you, my dearest Louisa.'

Louisa frowned.

'You are going to Ireland? But Master Cromwell is there!'

'Which is why he is going there,' The Countess of Derby interposed dryly. 'If someone doesn't stop that man in his tracks, there will be no peace for this land.'

'Then you plan to kill him?' Louisa asked, in an awestruck tone. 'Oh, but Papa! That will be a very dangerous mission!'

'I know that, which is why I will be going with him, seeing as I know more about Noll Cromwell's mode of behaviour,' Jocelyn answered for his brother.

'Oh Uncle Jocelyn, forgive me! I was so overcome to see Papa again that I haven't even asked you how you managed to survive a ducking in the Kitterland Straits!'

'I was picked up by the same fishing vessel as Armand,' Jocelyn Foster replied. 'We were very lucky, for several more minutes in that sea and we would have undoubtedly drowned.'

Louisa gave a mirthless laugh.

'Lucky!' she echoed. 'But think of poor Armand now, struck down by that monster, Magnus Stapleton's sword!'

The others glanced at one another, and then the Countess said, 'It has indeed been unfortunate, and we are all most distressed by it, but as I told you, Mam'selle, my nephew is having the best treatment possible, so I would ask you to try not to worry too much, and to take pleasure in your father and uncle's company while they are here.'

There was a slight rebuke in her voice which was not lost on Louisa, and she realised that she must at least try to show some pleasure in her father and uncle's presence. Oh, it wasn't that she was not pleased to see them — far from it — but she was so worried about Armand, that it was difficult to put thoughts of him from her head, and to feel pleasure actually made her guilty, when his life was still in danger.

'How long will you and Uncle Jocelyn be staying?' she asked her father now.

'As long as we can,' her father replied slightly enigmatically, and Louisa guessed that they would stay until it was clear what was going to become of Armand.

'You must see something of the island while you are here,' the countess said. 'For it is a beautiful place, with lush green hills and verdant valleys.'

'That would give us much pleasure,'

Jocelyn Foster said, bowing to her.

Charlotte smiled.

'And now I think we shall have some tea.' And she rang a bell on the wall to summon a maidservant. 'Look how anglicised I have become!' she exclaimed, clapping her plump hands. 'When I was in France I wouldn't have dreamed of drinking tea, but now to order it comes quite naturally to me!'

'No doubt it is the influence of your noble husband, the Earl James,' Sir Randolph said.

'Yes, methinks that it is,' Charlotte replied, a faraway look in her brown eyes, as she thought of the Earl, vainly struggling against the might of Parliament in England.

She sighed deeply.

'You must not think that you are on your own, Mam'selle Louisa, for we women all have our crosses to bear!'

★ ★ ★

During the next few days, Louisa, her father and uncle, accompanied by Jane, travelled all around the Isle of Man in a carriage loaned them by Charlotte Derby.

The weather was perfect, and it was, as the countess had said, a truly beautiful place. Louisa felt that she would have been perfectly happy, only for one thing, her concern for Armand.

She was still not permitted to visit him, and this in itself was purgatory to her, as any information she got about him was invariably second-hand. And she couldn't be sure whether the speaker was telling her the truth, or simply what he or she believed she wanted to hear.

Then, one morning, when she had just finished her toilette, having decided to dispense with the services of a maid and attend to herself, largely because she was feeling so dispirited that it was nice to spend some time alone, there was a tap at the door.

Louisa sighed.

No doubt it would be one of the servants coming to tell her that the countess had arranged yet another divertissement for her . . .

'Come in,' she called, her voice sounding weary even to her own ears.

The door opened and Jane came rushing into the room, a smile on her homely face.

Louisa looked at her in surprise.

'Why Jane! You look as if you're a cat who has just consumed a saucer of cream!'

'And so will you, when I tell you my news!'

Louisa felt her heart thumping wildly.

'Is it about Armand?' she asked, scarcely able to keep a tremor out of her voice.

'It is indeed!' Jane confirmed. 'And wonderful news it is too, for he is out of danger, and his principal physician, Dr Mandeville, who came with the Countess from France, has declared that you may go and see him directly!'

Louisa flung herself into Jane's arms,

nearly knocking the older woman off her feet.

'Oh, but that's marvellous! Oh Jane, I'm so happy! So very, very happy!'

'I thought you would be,' Jane replied, smiling.

'I'll go there right away, I know where his room is.' And Louisa headed for the door.

'Do you want me to come with you?'

'No, thank you Jane, this is something which I would like to do on my own.'

Jane nodded.

'Well don't tire him out,' she cautioned, 'for although he is making an excellent recovery, he will still be weak, and you know how boisterous you can be when you're happy, my love!'

'I won't!' Louisa promised and then she was out of the room and hurrying along the corridor in the direction of Armand's room.

* * *

She was dismayed when she saw him, for although he was propped up in bed, his formerly tanned skin was as white as the pillows he lay against. The smile he gave her, however, was sweet and loving, and he held out his hand to beckon her to come to his side.

Louisa didn't hesitate. She was by his bedside as fast as her slippered feet could carry her.

'My love, 'tis wonderful to see you,' he said. 'Will you sit down beside me, and then perhaps we can make up for the time that we've lost.'

Louisa sat down on a chair by the side of his bed.

'How are you feeling?' she asked, anxiety evident in her voice and eyes.

He laughed softly.

'A bit as if I've been kicked by a crazed stallion, which in some ways, I suppose I have! But I don't want to talk about myself, I want to talk about you, my dear Louisa. I have something to tell you, and that is that I think I've been in love with you since the first moment that I set eyes on you! The physician is confident that I should be able to leave my bed by tomorrow at the latest, and my dearest wish is to make you my wife just as soon as I am strong enough to walk down the aisle!'

Louisa was silent, her blue eyes looking at him in wonderment. Armand, however, didn't interpret her expression correctly, and became hesitant.

'Oh, Louisa! You're not angry with me, are you? Perhaps I have spoken of my feelings towards you too quickly, perhaps I . . . '

Louisa leaned forward and gently brushed her lips against his.

'Not at all, my love! You have spoken exactly as I had hoped you would, and I can assure you that your love is returned in plenty!'

'Then we must plight our troth,' he said, his dark eyes shining, as from under the bedclothes he produced a small, dark blue velvet covered ring box, and opened it to reveal a beautiful diamond and ruby betrothal ring. 'This belonged to my grandmother,' he said, taking her hand and placing the ring on her finger. 'See, it fits just as if it had been made for you!'

Louisa looked down at the ring.

'It's truly lovely,' she said admiringly. But then she couldn't quite prevent a slight shudder from rippling through her slim body, as she remembered the Roundhead commander who had wanted her for himself.

'What's the matter, my darling?' Armand's voice was anxious.

'I was just thinking about that brute of a fellow, Magnus Stapleton,' she said quietly.

Armand's dark brows drew together in a frown.

'He didn't hurt you in any way, did he, my love?'

Louisa shook her head.

'No, no!' Then she smiled grimly. 'Although I feel sure that he would have if I had been forced to go to Ireland! What happened to him, anyway?'

Armand shook his head.

'Oh, he survived! That one, I think is like the proverbial cat with nine lives! You know that I struck him quite hard with that boulder, and yet, somehow he managed to recover consciousness, hit the men who had been carrying him to the Royalist ship, and defy imprisonment in one of the dungeons here at the castle, and then headed off in the opposite direction at great speed!'

Louisa couldn't help but laugh. Magnus certainly did seem to bear a charmed life.

'He certainly had miraculous powers of survival! Do you think that he might be some sort of magician, like Merlin?'

'No, just a hard-headed lout!' Armand replied, his tone slightly sour, as he thought of the great hulk of a man who had been his rival. 'But let's not waste our time talking of that fellow.' His eyes darkened. 'Come here, Louisa, and give me a kiss.'

Louisa felt a tremor pass through her body.

'Are you sure that you're feeling strong enough?' she murmured.

Armand laughed, and reaching out, pulled her to him.

'That is up to you to find out!' he said, as he brought his lips down on hers.

THE END

Other titles in the Linford Romance Library

SAVAGE PARADISE
Sheila Belshaw

For four years, Diana Hamilton had dreamed of returning to Luangwa Valley in Zambia. Now she was back — and, after a close encounter with a rhino — was receiving a lecture from a tall, khaki-clad man on the dangers of going into the bush alone!

PAST BETRAYALS
Giulia Gray

As soon as Jon realized that Julia had fallen in love with him, he broke off their relationship and returned to work in the Middle East. When Jon's best friend, Danny, proposed a marriage of friendship, Julia accepted. Then Jon returned and Julia discovered her love for him remained unchanged.

PRETTY MAIDS ALL IN A ROW
Rose Meadows

The six beautiful daughters of George III of England dreamt of handsome princes coming to claim them, but the King always found some excuse to reject proposals of marriage. This is the story of what befell the Princesses as they began to seek lovers at their father's court, leaving behind rumours of secret marriages and illegitimate children.

THE GOLDEN GIRL
Paula Lindsay

Sarah had everything — wealth, social background, great beauty and magnetic charm. Her heart was ruled by love and compassion for the less fortunate in life. Yet, when one man's happiness was at stake, she failed him — and herself.

A DREAM OF HER OWN
Barbara Best

A stranger gently kisses Sarah Danbury at her Betrothal Ball. Little does she realise that she is to meet this mysterious man again in very different circumstances.

HOSTAGE OF LOVE
Nara Lake

From the moment pretty Emma Tregear, the only child of a Van Diemen's Land magnate, met Philip Despard, she was desperately in love. Unfortunately, handsome Philip was a convict on parole.

THE ROAD TO BENDOUR
Joyce Eaglestone

Mary Mackenzie had lived a sheltered life on the family farm in Scotland. When she took a job in the city she was soon in a romantic maze from which only she could find the way out.

NEW BEGINNINGS
Ann Jennings

On the plane to his new job in a hospital in Turkey, Felix asked Harriet to put their engagement on hold, as Philippe Krir, the Director of Bodrum hospital, refused to hire 'attached' people. But, without an engagement ring, what possible excuse did Harriet have for holding Philippe at bay?

THE CAPTAIN'S LADY
Rachelle Edwards

1820: When Lianne Vernon becomes governess at Elswick Manor, she finds her young pupil is given to strange imaginings and that her employer, Captain Gideon Lang, is the most enigmatic man she has ever encountered. Soon Lianne begins to fear for her pupil's safety.

THE VAUGHAN PRIDE
Margaret Miles

As the new owner of Southwood Manor, Laura Vaughan discovers that she's even more poverty stricken than before. She also finds that her neighbour, the handsome Marius Kerr, is a little too close for comfort.

HONEY-POT
Mira Stables

Lovely, well-born, well-dowered, Russet Ingram drew all men to her. Yet here she was, a prisoner of the one man immune to her graces — accused of frivolously tampering with his young ward's romance!

DREAM OF LOVE
Helen McCabe

When there is a break-in at the art gallery she runs, Jade can't believe that Corin Bossinney is a trickster, or that she'd fallen for the oldest trick in the book . . .

FOR LOVE OF OLIVER
Diney Delancey

When Oliver Scott buys her family home, Carly retains the stable block from which she runs her riding school. But she soon discovers Oliver is not an easy neighbour to have. Then Carly is presented with a new challenge, one she must face for love of Oliver.

THE SECRET OF MONKS' HOUSE
Rachelle Edwards

Soon after her arrival at Monks' House, Lilith had been told that it was haunted by a monk, and she had laughed. Of greater interest was their neighbour, the mysterious Fabian Delamaye. Was he truly as debauched as rumour told, and what was the truth about his wife's death?

THE SPANISH HOUSE
Nancy John

Lynn couldn't help falling in love with the arrogant Brett Sackville. But Brett refused to believe that she felt nothing for his half-brother, Rafael. Lynn knew that the cruel game Brett made her play to protect Rafael's heart could end only by breaking hers.

PROUD SURGEON
Lynne Collins

Calder Savage, the new Senior Surgical Officer at St. Antony's Hospital, had really lived up to his name, venting a savage irony on anyone who fell foul of him. But when he gave Staff Nurse Honor Portland a lift home, she was surprised to find what an interesting man he was.

A PARTNER FOR PENNY
Pamela Forest

Penny had grown up with Christopher Lloyd and saw in him the older brother she'd never had. She was dismayed when he was arrogantly confident that she should not trust her new business colleague, Gerald Hart. She opposed Chris by setting out to win Gerald as a partner both in love and business.

SURGEON ASHORE
Ann Jennings

Luke Roderick, the new Consultant Surgeon for Accident and Emergency, couldn't understand why Staff Nurse Naomi Selbourne refused to apply for the vacant post of Sister. Naomi wasn't about to tell him that she moonlighted as a waitress in order to support her small nephew, Toby.

A MOONLIGHT MEETING
Peggy Gaddis

Megan seemed to have fallen under handsome Tom Fallon's spell, and she was no longer sure if she would be happy as Larry's wife. It was only in the aftermath of a terrible tragedy that she realized the true meaning of love.

THE STARLIT GARDEN
Patricia Hemstock

When interior designer Tansy Donaghue accepted a commission to restore Beechwood Manor in Devon, she was relieved to leave London and its memories of her broken romance with architect Robert Jarvis. But her dream of a peaceful break was shattered not only by Robert's unexpected visit, but also by the manipulative charms of the manor's owner, James Buchanan.

THE BECKONING DAWN
Georgina Ferrand

For twenty-five years Caroline has lived the life of a recluse, believing she is ugly because of a facial scar. After a successful operation, the handsome Anton Tessler comes into her life. However, Caroline soon learns that the kind of love she yearns for may never be hers.

THE WAY OF THE HEART
Rebecca Marsh

It was the scandal of the season when world-famous actress Andrea Lawrence stalked out of a Broadway hit to go home again. But she hadn't jeopardized her career for nothing. The beautiful star was onstage for the play of her life — a drama of double-dealing romance starring her sister's fiancé.

VIENNA MASQUERADE
Lorna McKenzie

In Austria, Kristal Hastings meets Rodolfo von Steinberg, the young cousin of Baron Gustav von Steinberg, who had been her grandmother's lover many years ago. An instant attraction flares between them — but how can Kristal give her love to Rudi when he is already promised to another . . . ?

HIDDEN LOVE
Margaret McDonagh

Until his marriage, Matt had seemed like an older brother to Teresa. Now, five years later, Matt's wife has tragically died and Teresa feels she must go and comfort him. But how much longer can she hold on to the secret that has been hers for all these years?

A MOST UNUSUAL MARRIAGE
Barbara Best

Practically penniless, Dorcas Wareham meets Suzette, who tells her that she had rashly married a Captain Jack Bickley on the eve of his leaving for the Boer War. She suggests that Dorcas takes her place, saying that Jack didn't expect to survive the war anyway. With some misgivings, Dorcas finally agrees. But Jack does return . . .

A TOUCH OF TENDERNESS
Juliet Gray

Ben knew just how to charm, how to captivate a woman — though he could not win a heart that was already in another man's keeping. But Clare was desperately anxious to protect him from a pain she knew too well herself.

NEED FOR A NURSE
Lynne Collins

When Kelvin, a celebrated actor, regained consciousness after a car accident, he had lost his memory. He was shocked to learn that he was engaged to the beautiful actress Beth Hastings. His mind was troubled — and so was his heart when he became aware of the impact on his emotions of a pretty staff nurse . . .

WHISPER OF DOUBT
Rachel Croft

Fiona goes to Culvie Castle to value paintings for the owner, who is in America. After meeting Ewen McDermott, the heir to the castle, Fiona suspects that there is something suspicious going on. But little does she realise what heartache lies ahead of her . . .

MISTRESS AT THE HALL
Eileen Knowles

Sir Richard Thornton makes Gina welcome at the Hall, but his grandson, Zachary, calls her a fortune hunter. After Sir Richard's death, Gina finds taking over the role of Mistress at the Hall far from easy, and Zachary doesn't help — until he realises that he loves her.

PADLOCK YOUR HEART
Anne Saunders

Ignoring James Thornton's warning that it was cruel to give false hope, Faith set up a fund to send little Debby to Russia for treatment. Despite herself, Faith found she was falling in love with James. Perhaps she should have padlocked her heart against him.